M.V.P

HIS MOST VALUABLE PLAYER

MZ. LADY P.

M.V.P

Copyright by @ Mz. Lady P.

Published by: Shan Presents

www.shanpresents.com

SUBSCRIBE

Text Shan to 22828 to stay up to date with new releases, sneak peeks, contest, and more...

WANT TO BE A PART OF SHAN PRESENTS?

To submit your manuscript to Shan Presents, please send the first three chapters and synopsis to submissions@shanpresents.com

1

NI'YOKA "YOKA" CAMPBELL

I sat stone-faced in my car staring at the beautiful two-story home on the other side of the street. The house is not what stood out to me. It was my nigga's cocaine white Benz that sat in the driveway. After all the digging and snooping that I had been doing I was now regretting it. That saying "don't go looking for shit because you might get your feelings hurt" was so true. I was feeling stupid, and my feelings were so hurt. At first, I wanted to catch Zuri with this bitch that I had been hearing him sneak on the phone with and text often.

I had been with Zuri since my freshman year of college. At eighteen years old, I thought I had met my knight in shining armor. He was really a wolf in sheep's clothing that had the ability to charm a bitch right up out her panties. He was twenty-five, and my mother told me not to get involved with him. I should have listened, but I was captivated by a boss. That's exactly what Zuri was and still is. He's one of the biggest dope boys Georgia had ever seen. He was a legend in the south. Niggas feared him and bitches loved him.

I wiped the lone tear that had fallen from my face as I thought about how after five years we were still in the same place. I wasn't his wife, and we didn't have children. I've always been everything he needed me to be, but somehow I still fall short of having him fully. I kick my own ass every day for becoming comfortable with the disrespectful shit that he does. As long as I had him in any capacity, I was fine. He spoiled me and gave me everything I wanted. I have the house and the white picket fence. I just don't have the dog and the children that go along with it. I have one of the most extravagant houses in our subdivision. That's the problem. It's just a house with lavish shit inside of it, not a home.

"Come on, Yoka! Let's just leave." The sound of my best friend Seven's voice brought me out of my thoughts. She had got a new position at her job and moved down to Miami. I was so happy she had come to visit me. Being with her was like a breath of fresh air.

"I need to see him with her. I want to see what she looks like."

"I just don't understand why you want to subject yourself to this mental anguish. You know damn well you're one of the baddest bitches around these parts. Any bitch Zu fucks with is a mother-fucking downgrade. Just go home and wait for him to come. Address this situation in the privacy of your home. He's already got you out here looking bad."

I laid my head back on the headrest and closed my eyes. Seven was always the voice of reasoning, and she never sugar coated shit. That's why I fucked with her. She's that friend that is going to tell you what you need to hear and not what you wanted to hear.

"You're right. Let's get out of here."

As soon as I got ready to start the car, the door opened to the house he was inside of. I pulled my hat down over my eyes so that I couldn't be seen. Zu casually walked out, and a bitch stood in the doorway. My heart dropped when I saw her place her hand over her stomach. This bitch was pregnant. He went back towards her and kissed her passionately.

"Oh man, friend! I put my head down in my hands and cried like a baby.

"Why is he doing this to me?" I cried.

"Because you let him. Your ass is sitting here crying when you should be out there kicking his ass. I can't believe he's still fucking that bitch." Her last statement caught me off guard.

"Wait a minute. You know that bitch?"

"Look Yoka. I didn't want to say anything but Zu's been fucking with Da'Loni for a minute. I actually thought you knew about them the way they be out in the streets together. You would know that if you came out of that house that he makes you stay in so that he can whore around outside."

"How come you didn't tell me?"

"Honestly, I'm tired of telling you about your nigga cheating. It's a waste of time. You're not going to leave that nigga. Right now, you just saw some shit with your own eyes, and you're not going to leave. I'm really over all of this."

I sat quietly and took in everything in. I wasn't mad at Seven, but her choice of words hurt me. I chose not even respond. I waited until Zuri pulled off and a couple of seconds later I did the same. I dropped Seven off without so much as a word. I wasn't mad. I just didn't know what to say. Her words were dripping with the truth. It just hurts because she's my go-to person. I tell her everything about me. So, to know that she felt that way had me in my feelings. I just know now it's better for me to keep shit to myself.

When I pulled into the garage, Zuri's car was already inside. I took a deep breath before I went inside. I was trying to figure out what I was going to say to him or if I was going to confront him at all.

"Where you been at?"

"I went to the mall." I don't know why I said that. It was just the first thing that came to my mind.

"Where are the bags at?"

"I didn't find anything." I got ready to walk away, but he yanked me back by my hair and slammed me into the wall.

"Did you get what you were looking for today? Make that the last motherfucking time you follow me, Yoka. I'm glad you did follow me because now it's not so hard for me to tell you about my son that's on the way. I've tried being patient, but you can't have kids, and I need someone to carry on my legacy. Just think about it. You can now have the baby you always wanted. On the bright side, you don't have to go through all that pain of childbirth. Don't worry you're still the only woman for me. Let's lay down." He tried to push me towards the stairs, but I pushed him away from me.

"No! Are you serious right now? Do you really think I'm going to be okay with another bitch giving you a baby? I'll never play step momma to a bastard ass baby."

Before the words got out of my mouth good, he punched me so hard that it caused my head to bounce off the wall. I immediately fell to my knees and that when the blood from my nose started dripping on the white carpet. He grabbed me by the back of my neck and pressed my face into the blood-stained carpet.

"It's been a minute since I knocked the shit out of you, and that's the problem. Watch your motherfucking mouth. Don't come to bed until you get that blood out of the carpet." He casually walked up the stairs like it was nothing.

After about an hour of scrubbing the carpet, I was exhausted and ready to lay down. Zuri's gun case caught my attention as I got ready to head up the stairs. He had long ago bought me a Tiffany& Co diamond handled nine-millimeter gun, took me to the range, and taught me how to shoot and everything. I slowly opened the case so that he wouldn't hear me. I grabbed the gun and headed upstairs. I was numb, and I was hurting. When I walked inside of the room, he was asleep on his back. I mounted him and placed my gun to the middle of his forehead. His eyes popped open, and he looked like a deer caught in headlights.

"Come on now, Yoka baby! Put the gun down!" he pleaded.

"Do you love her?" I know I was looking ugly ass hell with my tears running down my face mixed with mascara. I was shaking and trembling so much that I couldn't even keep the gun steady.

"You know I don't love nobody but you. Put the gun down, Yoka."

"How could you do this to me, Zu? I've given you five years of my life. I stood by you when you've needed me the most, and now you're blatantly telling me that I have to accept your son with another woman.

"You don't have to accept anything Yoka, but you're going to because you love me. Now put the gun down so we can talk about this," he softly spoke as he finessed the gun out of my hands.

As soon as it was out my reach, I immediately got me up off of him. I tried running away, but he grabbed me by my hair basically slamming me onto the hardwood floor. The impact knocked the wind out of me, and I could barely breathe.

"This is what the fuck you like, huh? Don't ever pull a mother-fucking gun on a real nigga. You got me fucked up. It doesn't feel good to have a motherfucking gun pointed in your face, do it? I should shoot your motherfucking ass right now for playing with me. You gone pay for that stunt your bitch ass just pulled."

I watched as he threw on some clothes and left out of the bedroom. I continued to lay in the same spot crying my heart out. After everything that we had accomplished together, I couldn't believe he would do me like this. I've always been the good girl. I've never cheated, lied, or did anything to make him question my loyalty. For hours, I tried to figure out if it was something that I did and didn't remember. I came up with nothing because I hadn't done anything wrong.

∼

IT HAD BEEN a week since I saw or heard from Zu. I knew that he was alive and well because I had drove past the spots where he and his crew hung at. I wanted to beg him to come home, but I couldn't bring myself to do that. My dumb ass had already shown him just how weak I was over him. The walls of my life were starting to close in on me, and I felt like I was spiraling out of control. I couldn't talk to Seven because she was tired of hearing the shit. I wasn't mad at her because I was tired of telling her anyway. At this point, I was embarrassed to even tell her any more of what was going on. Although she was my best friend and I knew she loved me, there is just some shit you just have to keep to yourself.

I wanted so badly to call my mother and talk to her, but she would tell me that she told me so. That's the last thing that I wanted to hear at the moment. She never approved of our relationship, and I she made sure to let it be known. Since I couldn't bring myself to go home and talk to my mother, I found myself at Zu's momma house. We had such a good relationship, and she had been the best mother-in-law a girl could ask for.

When I pulled up to her house, there were tons of cars in the driveway. There were blue balloons tied outside to the fence. The entire front of the house was draped in baby shower directions. My heart was beating rapidly as I walked inside of the house.

"Aww!" was all I heard as I headed to the living room where voices could be heard.

When I rushed inside, I felt like my soul had left my body. Zu's entire family was sitting around watching as he and Da'Loni opened baby gifts. The entire room stopped what they were doing when they realized I was standing there. I was numb and speechless. My mind was trying to process the scene before me. I've always had such a good relationship with his family. Granted they worshipped Zu and he was their blood but damn. These are the same people who I've partied with, ate with, and spent holidays with. It's funny how his sisters called me their sister. The shit hurt my heart so bad that I felt like I was dying.

"Really Zuri?"

"Go home, Yoka."

"Nooooo! Please talk to me," I cried, and I know that I looked pitiful as fuck to everyone, but I didn't care.

"Go ahead and talk to her. She's ruining the shower your family is giving me." Zuri rubbed her stomach and walked towards me. He grabbed me by the collar of my shirt and basically dragged me out of the house.

"Why Zuri! Just tell me what I did. Please! Tell me something. How can you do this to me?" Zuri quickly grabbed me and held me to keep me from falling. I had lost the will to stand up.

"Go home, Yoka. You already know about the baby. There is no need for you to come over here performing acting all surprised and shit."

"What the fuck do you mean? Last time I checked you were my man, not hers!"

"Your man is my man!" that bitch sang like she was SZA as she stood on the porch, and I immediately tried to go after her.

"Bitch, you done lost your mind!" Zuri said as he grabbed me back. He dragged me by my hair towards my car, causing me to lose my balance.

"That's enough, Zuri! You don't manhandle her like that. I don't give a fuck what's going on. Don't you ever put your hands on her like that again! Everybody go inside of the house now, including you, Zuri!"

"Man, Ma! This is my woman, and I know how to handle Yoka!"

"Oh, this is your woman? Last time I checked you were in my house with your side bitch at your baby shower. Get the hell out of my face, Zuri! I told you I didn't want this bullshit at my house. As a matter of fact, this shit is over. Pack up your gifts and get the fuck out." His mother waited until everyone walked back into the house before grabbing me into her embrace.

"Why is he doing me like this, Ms. Zora? I didn't do anything."

"That's the problem, Yoka. You allow Zu to treat you like shit. How many times are you going to forgive him? This nigga is having a baby shower right now, and you aren't the mother. I'm not trying to be rude, but damn, do I have to pull out the dumb bitch flash cards to get you to see what I'm saying. That's my son, and I love him, but I'm a woman before I'm anything. Get in your car and leave his ass. Go and regain your dignity because you've given it all to him. I love you Yoka, but you deserve better than this. I'm sorry that you had to come to my home and see this. As a mother, I'm embarrassed and ashamed of my son's behavior. Please leave, Yoka. I don't want you to hurt any more than you already are."

I wanted to scream, curse, and fight. However, what would it do? After acting a fool, he would still have a baby on the way with another woman. In my heart, I knew I could never accept it. As I drove away, I let the tears flow. Memories of the happier times flashed in my head. That shit only made me cry harder. I had built a life with this man. Everything I had accomplished I did it with him. The fact that he was saying fuck me for no reason at all had a bitch fucked up mentally. For a second, I thought about killing myself. That was when I knew that I needed to walk away from Zu. It was obvious what we had was over and done with anyway. Instead of going to the house we shared, I left everything behind in Georgia. I had money in my personal account that could definitely allow me to start over. Fuck all of that material shit. Here I was with a fucking master's degree in Business and have never done anything with it. My dumb ass graduated and have been sitting on my ass reaping the benefits of my drug dealing ass nigga. It's all good though because I guarantee you Zuri "Zu" Johnson will regret the day he fucked over me.

MIDWAY TO FLORIDA, I realized that my dumb ass should have filled up before jumping on the highway. As I stood pumping the gas, I couldn't help but shed tears like a motherfucker.

"Damn, lil baby! You ugly as fuck crying like that. Here, wipe them tears. I know under all that snot and mascara you're beautiful. With a body like that, you have to have a face to match it."

I wanted to curse this nigga out for that ugly comment, but he had me in awe. This nigga was fine as fuck. He had me the moment he flashed a mouth full of gold.

"Thank you." I took the napkins he handed me and wiped my face.

"You're so fucking pretty now. What's your name, love?"

"I'm Ni'yoka."

"I'm Sheikem, but you can call me Sheik. He winked at me and handed me a card before jumping in his Porsche. Gucci ain't never lied when he said, *Miss one next fifteen one coming!!*

I quickly shook that thought from my mind because the last thing I should be doing is thinking about another man. After I finished pumping my gas, my stomach started to growl, so I walked back into the gas station to get me some snacks. As I walked towards the coolers, there were two niggas engaged in a conversation. Of course, my nosey ass decided to ear hustle.

"That was that nigga Sheik! I swear we should run down on that nigga now. He ain't that far up the road that we can't catch up with his bitch ass."

"I thought y'all squashed that beef?"

"That's what I want that nigga to think! That nigga tried to handle me like I was a bitch or something. There ain't no expiration date on disrespect. Fuck all that talking! I'm about to try and get at that nigga now!"

My heart started racing as I saw the nigga rush out of the gas station. I don't know why, but I felt the need to rush out of the door as well. As I speed walked, I reached into my back pocket and grabbed my cell phone. When the niggas jumped inside the car, I quickly took pictures of the license plates. When they pulled off, I waited, and then I pulled off.

I know that I don't know Sheik, but I definitely didn't want it on my conscious if he was hurt or even worse killed. Remembering I had his card, I pulled it from my pocket and quickly called him. After several attempts, I left him a voicemail telling him to get in contact with me. At the same time, I didn't even realize that the car in front of me stopped short until it was too late.

SHEIKEM "SHEIK" SHAKUR

After a long ass drive from Georgia back to Florida, I was more than ready to lay it the fuck down. This would be my last month riding down to see my best friend and brother Hussein. He had been gone for two years, and next month he's coming home. At twenty-five, these people thought that I was never going to be able to keep our drug and gun running business afloat, but I've proved every motherfucking body wrong. Not only did it flourish, but it has expanded from state to state. Not to mention over the last couple of years I've managed to open up a chain of restaurants and nightclubs that have done amazing.

As soon as I walked inside of my home, I wanted to walk the fuck out. My wife Azada and her ghetto ass friends were loud as fuck. It's not even five o' clock, and these bitches are drunk as fuck. She was so engrossed in entertaining her friends that she never even heard me come into the house. That shit was cool with me because I didn't feel like being bothered with anyone. I work hard as hell and can't even come home to a hot meal. The worst mistake I ever could have made with Azada was spoiling her rotten and not making that bitch treat me like the king I am. I'm already knowing we won't be married too much longer. This bitch ain't trying to change, and I'm not trying to teach no grown bitch how to treat her husband. One thing for sure and two for certain, the next bitch is gone have to come as a finished product.

"Hey, babe! I didn't know you were here!" she screamed loudly.

That irritated me because she knows I hate a loud bitch. Women are made to be seen and not heard. Now don't get me wrong when I say that. I more so mean that a woman should be ladylike at all times. Women should always speak in a respectful tone. Don't no nigga want no loud ass bitch acting like a ghetto ass bird.

"Fuck you so loud for?"

"Damn! Who pissed in your cornflakes? You've been gone all weekend, and you come home with an attitude for no reason." I shook my head at Azada because this bitch didn't have a clue, and she for damn sure couldn't buy a fucking vowel.

"Get your drunk ass out of here. A nigga is tired as fuck, and I need to get up in a couple of hours." I waved her ass off, undressed, and got in bed. I didn't give a fuck what Azada did. I just wanted her to get the fuck out of my sight.

"I don't even know why I try with your ass."

"That's because your ass is trying instead of actually doing. Instead of shopping and entertaining them user ass friends of yours, start cleaning this motherfucker up instead of paying people to do it. Cook for a nigga instead of always ordering take out. Stop drinking day in and day out. Maybe then your pussy wouldn't be dry as the fucking Sahara Desert."

I could look into her eyes and tell that I hurt her feelings, but I didn't give a fuck. Sometimes you have to hurt these bitches' feelings in order to shed light on their bullshit. I turned my back on her ass to let her know I was finished talking. She could miss me with them tears. The truth was that even though I had said that to her she wouldn't change a thing.

Instead of doing what I told her she should be doing, she's going to instead grab my bank cards and shop. I wouldn't stop her because it's more money where that came from. Plus, I'm no selfish nigga. I love for my bitch to look good. I also love for my bitch to love me pass my money and status. Sadly, after three years that's all she sees me as. I won't say she doesn't love me because I know that she does. I just know the motive is the money with Azada. She thrives on wearing Gucci, Yves St. Laurent, Prada, and Christian Louboutin's just so she can show off to her ghetto ass friends. She better hope that all of that materialistic shit keeps her warm at night because I'm fed the fuck up.

Hours later, I listened to my voicemails and became perplexed when a damn nurse was talking about my sister was in a car accident. That shit was a stone cold lie because I didn't have no fucking sister. At the same time, it had piqued my interests to see who the fuck would be in the hospital claiming to be my damn sister. Whoever the fuck it is better have a good ass reason why they want to lie about being kin to me. I don't fuck with many people, so I'm lost as to why someone would want to play with their own life.

~

"I'M SHEIKEM SHAKUR. I received a call that my sister was in an accident," I spoke to the clerk in the emergency room.

"Oh yes. Your sister gave us your number. Here is a visiting pass. She's back there in bed six." The lady handed me the pass and buzzed me in the door.

I quickly walked until I found bed six. Needless to say, I was shocked when I pulled the curtains back looking at the chick with the ugly ass cry back at the gas station. She had a patch on her head with blood seeping through it. Other than that, she was awake. Her eyes grew wider seeing me standing there.

"Are you crazy or some shit? Why the fuck would you tell these people you're my sister?"

"Look, I know how this may look, but I needed to talk to you. Earlier today, when you left out of the gas station, I overheard some guys talking about killing you. They even went so far as to get in their car and try to catch up with you. That's how I ended up getting into a wreck. I was trying to call you on the phone and let you know. I took my eyes off the road for a second, and that's how I ended up slamming into the car in front of me. I'm sorry."

I was still looking at this chick like she was crazy because she didn't know me from a can of paint. It was not a good idea for her to go behind some niggas who was trying to get at me." As I stood in deep thought, she handed me her phone. I immediately knew who the fuck it was when I saw the car. These niggas just didn't know when to let shit go.

"That was stupid as hell what you did. You could have lost your life behind a nigga you didn't even know. At the same time, I appreciate that shit. That was some real ass shit to do for a stranger. I would like to pay you for doing that. How much do you want?"

"I don't want your money, Sheikem. I just want you to apologize for calling me ugly." I couldn't do shit but laugh.

"Are you serious right now?"

"Don't laugh nigga because I'm dead ass serious right now." I had every intention of getting the fuck out of here when I realized who it was, but now this woman had me pulling up a damn chair.

"The only way I'll tell you sorry is if you tell me why you were crying in the first damn place." She looked surprised at what I said, but she realized that I was so serious.

"I found out that the nigga I loved for the last five years has a baby on the way by someone else. I guess it hurts because he's basically been in a relationship with the chick. I swear I think it hurts more because I can't have kids."

I saw her eyes water, and I immediately regretted asking. The last thing I wanted her to do was to be sad."

"Okay now stop all of that. I'm sorry for calling your crybaby ass ugly. Stop crying over that fuck nigga and boss up lil baby. Look, I need to get out here, but I appreciate you looking out for me, pretty girl. Get you some rest and hit me up if you need anything. I owe you big time."

I had to get the fuck out of the room quick. I was a nigga that didn't know how to handle that emotional shit. At the same time, I was more concerned about these bitch ass niggas that's out here plotting on me. I had been giving that gunplay a rest, but it's always a nigga that you have to remind just who you are. Yeah, I'm gone have to get this nigga Trick.

3

YOKA

Each and every time I looked at my forehead I get mad. It had been a month since the accident, and the scar on my forehead was taking forever to heal. I was happy as hell I had finally gotten the courage to reach out to Seven. The shit that had happened with Zuri had me all in my feelings. I literally just wanted to get on my shit out here in Florida. I didn't want to have to call my parents or Seven for anything. That's my best friend, but I no longer wanted to burden her with my issues. She was so disappointed in me behind dealing with Zuri's shit.

Now that I've moved into my condo and it's finally furnished, I'm ready to see what Miami has to offer me. I've deleted all of my social media pages and changed my number on Zuri's ass. I've even gone so far as to change all of my emails. When I say that I'm done with that motherfucker, I mean it.

Zuri is a fuck nigga, and I hate that it took for him to hurt me for me to see it.

It's only been a month since I've been away from his ass, and I feel so refreshed. This short time that I've had alone has given me peace of mind. I sleep so fucking good not thinking about where he at and who he's with. Any woman that has ever had to deal with a cheating ass nigga knows that feeling. I now know what Destiny's Child meant when they sang, *ain't no feeling like being free.* I feel free as a bird. A bitch is on a whole new level. Zuri who?"

I had been walking around my condo showing it off to Seven. I had finally gotten the nerve to tell her that I was now living in her neck of the woods. To say that she was shocked would be an understatement. I was every name in the book when I finally came clean.

"I still can't believe you've been out here all of this time and didn't tell me. You're so wrong for this shit. Zuri has been going crazy looking for you. I had to block that nigga when he started getting disrespectful. Something is seriously wrong with that motherfucker. He's lucky he wasn't standing in front of me because I would have sliced the shit out of him. That nigga is touched in the head. I'm happy as hell you're away from that psycho motherfucker."

"Fuck Zu! I'm sorry friend, but I just needed to get my mind right. The next time I saw you I wanted to be in my right state of mind. The last time we talked, you had said some shit that hit me. I never want you to look at me as a weak ass bitch behind no nigga. The truth is I was weak as fuck behind him. It took for him to treat me like shit in front of his entire family in order for me to see things clearly. When I walked into his mother's house, and they were having a baby shower for that bitch, my eyes opened up real quick. That added with him putting his hands on me for some time now put the icing on the cake. I jumped on the highway and left him and everything I owned behind. I'm sorry I just needed to work on me before I reached out to you." I quickly wiped my tears, and we hugged one another.

"I'm so glad you came out here. Now we can get out here in these Miami streets and see what the hype is about. As a matter of fact, we're going out tonight and turn the fuck up.

"No! I can't. I have to go and look at some spaces for my boutique. My mom knows this dope real estate agent who is going to look out for me on the prices, so I have to be on point. Bitch, I can't be late or show up drunk. I need a rain check on that shit. My mother would kill me. Now that I'm no longer with Zu, she's more than willing to invest in my company."

"Well, let's at least meet up for dinner. My bitch has finally left her nigga from hell, and we're going to celebrate that shit no matter what."

"Okay cool. Text me the location of the restaurant, and I'll meet you there. I'm telling you now I'm not getting fucked up!" I yelled at her as she rushed out of the door. If it were up to Seven, I would be drinking Hennessy out of the bottle with a damn straw. I'm not built for that shit.

I picked out what I was going to wear to dinner and took a much-needed nap once Seven left. Although I couldn't turn up like I wanted to, I was excited about getting out. The walls of my house were starting to close in on me. Some fresh air would do me good.

"Bitch, you lied. This is not no damn restaurant."

"They serve food hoe on the upper level. Right now we're about to get some drinks and chill the fuck out."

I rolled my eyes at this bitch because she had tricked the shit out of me. Instead of worrying about my appointment in the morning, I decided just to enjoy myself.

"Come on, bitch. I got us a section."

As we walked over to the section, my heart raced as I noticed the dude that was back at the gas station plotting on Sheik. I was so mad I didn't lock his number in my phone. Then again, I needed to mind my damn business. I still be having headaches since I hit my fucking head. When the waitress came with a bottle of Rémy and a gold bottle of Belaire, I just knew I was going to be fucked up. The waitress poured us a shot of Rémy and a glass of champagne.

"Fuck it! Let's toast to new beginnings in Miami!" I screamed.

As soon as we knocked our drinks back, the sound of rapid gunfire caused both of us to fall on the floor. When I looked up from the floor, two niggas dressed in all black was airing out the section of niggas that we had previously passed. Once they were satisfied with their work, they rushed out of the club. The main guy who was talking the shit back at the gas station was laid out on the floor with his brains next to him. I guess his luck had run out.

"Come on, bitch!" Seven snatched my ass up from the floor, and we hauled ass getting out of there.

I did not move down here to be in the middle of no damn shootouts. It was feeling like I was in Chiraq. That's my cue to stay my dumb ass in the house and get this money. Seven might as well chop it up cause this was my first and last time clubbing it with her ass.

4

SEVEN SANTANA

I sat in the distance all in my feelings as I watched Hussein and his wife Kimora enjoying themselves at his coming home party. It was like a dagger to my heart each and every time I watched him love on her. I guess it hurts more because I thought maybe after everything I had done for him, he would come around and finally love me. If he noticed me here he would have a fit, but what did he expect. Before he got locked up, we fucked around heavy. That's because Kimora was locked up for a gun charge that she had taken for him. When she was coming out, he was going in to serve a two-year sentence. While he's been away, I've visited a couple of times, and we've exchanged letters. I even went so far as to put money on his books, even though he didn't need it. Something inside of me just wanted him to know that I was riding for him. That's some stupid ass shit there because after it's all said and done, he's with his wife, and they look happy.

After ordering a couple of more drinks, I went to the bathroom before heading home. As I walked inside of the bathroom, I wanted to walk right back out, but I had to piss too bad. Kimora and some of her crew were standing there taking selfies. I brushed passed them and went into one of the available stalls. Seconds later, I came out to see this bitch leaning up against the sink.

"I know who you are. Stay away from my husband. There is nothing you could ever do for him that I can't. What you and he had is over? Trust me. You don't want to fuck with me." Before I could respond, some women rushed into the bathroom, and she walked out.

I don't give a fuck if Hussein is her husband or not. That's her first and last time ever thinking she is going to check me. That interaction alone lets me know that I don't need to be trying to fuck with Hussein. My days of beating bitches up over their man are over. I'm actually ready to settle down and have a family to call my own. I'm damn near thirty, and all I've done is party, bullshit, and work my ass off to get the things I want.

～

"WHAT THE HELL is wrong with you? I've been talking to you for the last five minutes, and I feel like you aren't listening to me."

"I'm sorry. A bitch mind was somewhere else. What were you saying?"

Yoka and I were sitting at Olive Garden having dinner. Ever since I had seen Hussein, my mind had been consumed by thoughts of him. I think what was really bothering me was the fact that he acted as if I wasn't even in the room. We locked eyes, and he quickly turned away. I didn't know how to feel about that. On the one hand, my feelings were hurt. On the other hand, I felt stupid as fuck. I mean what the fuck did I expect from the nigga. He was with his wife.

"Never mind I refuse to repeat that shit all over again."

"So, how is everything going with your boutique?"

"That shit is at a standstill for now. My mother had invested in it, but when she realized that she wasn't going to be in control, she took her money back. I don't have time for that shit. I'll do the shit myself. I love my mother, but she's petty as fuck. She's always being manipulative and throwing shit up in my face. She had the nerve to tell me I needed to bring my ass back to Atlanta. Talking about Zuri has moved on and not thinking about me. She has lost her fucking mind. That nigga don't care who he's with. He still wants to rule me with an iron fist. I'm good on going back to Atlanta."

"I'm so scared for you. I really think that you need to go and at least file a police report. You need to create a paper trail on his nutty ass."

Although Yoka had moved out here, I wasn't so sure Zuri wouldn't come and try getting her. His emails were threatening and convincing as fuck. That nigga was not done with Yoka.

"Zuri is not about to come all the way out here. That nigga is more so waiting for me to come back home. That will never happen, so he might as well continue living his happily ever after with his baby momma." I sipped my wine and didn't even speak on the subject any longer.

For the rest of our dinner, I drifted off periodically. My mind was all over Hussein. I felt bad that I couldn't tell Yoka about him. The shit was too embarrassing. Yoka was my best friend, so I knew she wouldn't judge me. However, she would get on me about fucking with a married man in the first place. Sometimes we as women hate to hear that real shit. We would rather have those friends that agree with everything we do. That's how I know Yoka is a true friend. She lets me know when I'm fucking up. Right now, I don't want to hear that, so it's best I keep the shit to myself.

~

"WHAT'S UP SEVEN, BABY?" I rolled my eyes, looking at Hussein sitting on the hood of his Porsche. I had just ended my shift and was headed towards my car in the hospital garage.

"What's good, Hussein?"

"Why haven't you been answering for a nigga?"

"Cause I blocked you. Plus, I don't think it's a good idea we continue talking anyway. Apparently, your wife doesn't like it." I tried opening my car door, but he blocked me.

"My wife isn't any of your concern. You knew I had a wife when we started this shit. I thought we were having fun."

"I'm too grown for games, Hussein. Maybe your wife likes that shit, but I don't. Now move out of my way. I'm tired, and all I want to do is go home and lay down." He stepped to the side, and I quickly hopped in my car and got the fuck out of dodge. That shit didn't matter because he followed me home and practically barged his way in.

Before I knew it, he had me bent over my chaise fucking the shit out of me. I couldn't fight him off even if I wanted to. His dick game was official, and with each stroke, I realized how much I missed this shit. As we fucked, I enjoyed the moment because I knew that when he left, I would feel stupid as fuck. No man should have this type of power over a woman. Not even a bossed up, sexy, handsome, and paid ass nigga like Hussein.

5

YOKA

I was so angry with my momma for doing the shit that she was doing to me. This woman wants to run my life, and I refuse to let her. Before I become her puppet, I'll struggle first. It was a good thing I had a hefty bank account from stealing out of Zuri's account. He has more money than he knows what to do with, so he won't miss it. Each and every time he put his hand on me, I subtracted a thousand dollars. For every time I caught him cheating or talking to some bitch, I taxed that ass twenty-five hundred. Just thinking about the shit made me mad, so I quickly shook it off.

I had been staying in the house in an effort not to spend any money on frivolous shit. I'm the type of person who needs a new outfit and shoes for every occasion. Now that I'm on a budget, I can't be doing that. At the same time, the walls of my house were starting to close in on me, so I decided to head out to South Beach just to relax by the water and chill for the weekend. I didn't even call Seven. The last time we were together her ass was off. That added with the fact that she hasn't really been reaching out to me. I know it's not a personal thing. She might just need some time to herself. I'll give her that because I've definitely been there before.

I was bored as hell as I walked down Ocean Drive. My ass was a tad bit self-conscious as I walked in my two-piece bathing suit. I had put on so much weight that my ass was spilling out of it. It was a good thing I had on my wrap. I made it to Fat Tuesdays and walked inside to get me something to drink. As soon as I walked inside, I noticed Sheik surrounded with bitches and niggas. I quickly turned my head as I stood in line to order my drink.

"What can I get you?"

"I would like to have a thirty-two-ounce strawberry with an extra shot."

As I stood and waited for my drink, I hope and prayed Sheik didn't see me. I didn't understand why I didn't want him to see me. Maybe it was just because I was self-conscious about the way that I was looking. My ass was out here damn near naked, and I just didn't want him to see me like that. Plus, the shit was super weird. He may think I'm a stalker or something.

After getting my drink, I headed towards the beach. Once I rented me some towels and an umbrella, I relaxed and chilled. This Florida air and palm trees got me feeling like I would never go back to Atlanta. The shit was so relaxing.

After about two hours and that damn drink, I was tired as fuck. It was a good thing I rented me a room at the Clevelander because it wasn't far from where I was on the beach. As soon as I made it to my room, I hopped in the shower and went right to sleep.

～

"I STILL CAN'T BELIEVE your ass has been down here without me."

"Look, bitch I needed to clear my head, and I wasn't about to call your Debbie Downer ass. The last time we went out, your ass was in another place."

I continued to put my makeup on as I got ready to go to some damn party Seven wanted me to go to. After my long ass nap, I woke up to damn near thirty missed calls and messages from her ass. The bitch was already in South Beach trying to go to some big hood nigga party. I actually didn't want to go after the last fiasco, but I'm going so that we can have some fun.

"Bitch, I'm sorry. I was going through some shit. We're best friends, and we never keep secrets from one another. However, it's this nigga named Hussein I had been fucking with. My ass has fallen in love with him, and he's married. Like, this nigga got me feeling some type of way. He just came home from prison after doing a short bid. We had been rocking prior to that because his wife was locked up. When she came home, he had to go in. They're both out now, and I don't like how he's handling me. This nigga showed up at my house, fucked me senseless, and dipped on my ass. I haven't heard from his dog ass since then. So, that's why I'm going to his brother's birthday party."

I shook my head listening to this crazy ass fool. Seven was about to cut up, but I'm with her right or wrong. At the same time, what the hell did she expect fucking with a married man?

"Well, you know I'm down to ride with you bitch. At the same time, don't expect nothing major from his dog ass. If he ain't trying to leave that bitch, then handle him like a side nigga. Don't let him treat you like a side bitch. You're wife material. Now, come on. Let's go see what's to this nigga."

"That's why I love you bitch because you gone give it to me raw."

"I love you bitch, but play this shit as cool as possible."

Seven is known for scrapping with niggas and bitches with no problem. Every fight I've ever been in has been because of her ass. That's my bitch though, so I'm down for whatever.

AFTER ABOUT ANOTHER hour we were at the Fontainebleau Hotel. The party was being held on one of their outside decks. Bitches were damn near naked, and I was feeling overdressed. As Seven and I grabbed a drink, we sat down in one of the cabanas. The crowd started going crazy, and that made both Seven and me jump up. I had to take a closer look when I realized it was Sheik and another fine ass nigga that kind of looked like him. The guy with him was holding a female's hand.

"That motherfucker!" My heart was beating fast cause I just knew she was talking about Sheik.

"That's him?"

"Yeah that's Hussein, and that's his wife, Kimora. I should have known that bitch was going to be here." I breathed a sigh of relief because although there was nothing between him and me, I was kind of digging him.

"He fine as fuck friend, I see why you dick silly off his ass. I actually know the nigga that's with him. Remember I was telling you about the incident at the gas station. Well, that's him. That's Sheik."

I grabbed another glass of champagne from the waitress and went back and sat down. Seven was still standing in outside of it looking in their direction.

"Excuse me can you send a bottle of Rémy over to the birthday boy's table. Let him know it from Seven." I shook my head in disbelief cause this bitch was about to embarrass us and get us put the fuck up out of here.

"Bitch, you crazy!" I couldn't help but laugh at her ass. At the same time, I couldn't keep my eyes of Sheik. He was looking so fucking good in his all-white linen suit with Gucci loafers. My pussy was getting wet just looking at him. I'm not sure what God is trying to tell me, but there has to be a reason why I keep running into this man.

"I'm not crazy. Hussein has to know that he can't keep playing with me and think shit is sweet."

Seven and I sat and watched in the distance as the waitress placed the bottle in front of them. She pointed them in our direction letting them know that the bottle came from our table. I took a huge sip of my drink as I Sheik and I locked eyes. My ass hurried up and looked away. The last thing I wanted him to think was that I was some type of stalker. Hussein's wife tried to walk towards us, but he stopped her. Instead, he came over, and I knew shit was about to get real.

"Let me talk to you for a minute!" Hussein gritted and yanked her up by her elbow, but she yanked away.

"Get your hands off of me, nigga!"

"I will fuck you up in here, Seven. Get your ass up right now!"

"You might as well fuck me up now!" Seven continued to sit and sip her champagne like it was nothing. At this point, Hussein realized she wasn't moving.

"Look, I don't understand why the fuck you doing this to yourself. You knew from the jump I was a married man. I've never given you the inkling that I would leave my wife. At the same time, I fucks with you hard. I'm all for this thing we have going on, but if you can't play your part, then I can't fuck with you at all, Seven baby. Go home, and I'll come over later so that we can talk about this shit. Right now, it's my wife's birthday party, and this whole set up is disrespectful. If it were the other way around, I would feel the same way." He kissed her on the forehead and walked away. Seven was just sitting with tears in her eyes. As much as I wanted to get on her about lying to me about whose birthday it really was, I decided not to. Instead, I reached over, and I hugged her.

"Let's just get out of here, friend. This party whack as fuck anyway."

"I'm not going anywhere. Fuck him, his wife, and this party."

"Why do you want to sit here and embarrass yourself like this? That man told you to leave his wife's party. Stop sitting here trying to prove a point to a nigga that don't give a fuck about you. While you are sitting here, that nigga is over there celebrating his wife's birthday. Don't be no fool over this nigga, Seven."

"You mean like you were over Zuri. All of a sudden, you're the voice of reason when it comes to leaving a nigga. Save me that self-righteous bullshit. I'm good."

I couldn't believe this bitch had just taken it there with me. I refused to even entertain her petty ass. Instead, I didn't respond. I grabbed my clutch and left her dumb ass sitting there. Seven and I have said some fucked up shit to one another in the past, so I'm not tripping. We'll be back talking tomorrow like nothing ever happened, but right now I have no words for the dick silly bitch.

I'm sorry, Yoka! Damn!" she yelled, but I stuck up my middle finger high as fuck. I was in my feelings at this point, and she could kiss my ass until I was ready to talk to her dumb ass. As I walked away, I prayed I didn't fall in these damn high heels. I stopped for a minute and removed them from my feet.

"I know your pretty ass not about to walk barefoot. That's thot shit." I looked up to Sheik, and I continued to remove my shoes. Fuck what he was talking about. My damn feet were hurting.

"I'm far from a thot. These damn shoes got my feet hurting."

I continued towards the elevator, and he did as well. I was trying my best to play it cool, but my heart was beating out of my chest. It was something about him that made me nervous. It's crazy because when I first met him, I didn't have that feeling. I guess it's because I didn't look at him like I do now. The shit started when he came to the hospital. He was so attentive and mesmerizing. I guess that was because I hadn't experienced that with a man in a long time.

"I guess you can keep them off since you have some beautiful as toes. Why are you leaving your friend?

"Thank you. I'm not leaving her. This is where she wants to be. I'm good though."

"She done came and got my brother in trouble. That party is officially over. Since we're both leaving, why don't you come to my suite and chill with a nigga? I promise I won't bite you."

"That's a good thing since I'm very sensitive."

"Is that right?" He said as we stepped off the elevator on what I guess was his floor. My cell phone was buzzing, but I didn't even bother to pull it out of my clutch. It wasn't nobody but Seven, and I was not fucking with her.

As he put the key card in, I decided to shut the bitch completely off.

"This is a really nice view of the beach."

"Ain't it though. That sunset is everything. Come on, let's sit on the balcony and chill. You smoke."

"Yeah, I do."

"Well here, roll these up for me."

It had been a minute since I rolled a blunt, but I knew I still had it in me. Zuri hated for me to smoke, so I used to have to sneak and do it when he wasn't home. As I separated the weed and broke the swishers down, Sheik stared at me intensely.

"What are you looking at?"

"You can roll a blunt, and you're beautiful, with pretty toes too. That's a lethal combination."

"Boy, stop it!"

We both laughed as I finished rolling. He grabbed a bottle of Rémy from the fridge and poured us both a cup. He grabbed my hand, and we went and sat out on the balcony. I was surprised with the whole grabbing of the hand thing. At the same time, he had the softest hands I had ever felt. That shit made me wonder what he did for a living.

Whatever it was, I knew it had to be lucrative cause he definitely had a taste for the finer things that life had to offer.

"What do you do for a living?"

"You're a nosey little fucker, aren't you?" I couldn't do shit but laugh because he was dead ass serious.

"I'm saying. Your hands are super soft. I just wondered what you did for a living. It's like you never get your hands dirty.

"That's true, beautiful. I never get my hands dirty unless necessary. Now pass the blunt. You're fucking up the rotation."

"You're so rude."

He opened his shirt and the words "RUDE BOY" was tatted across his chest. If that wasn't sexy enough, he had a six-pack out of this world. I don't know what Sheik was trying to do to me, but whatever the fuck it was, it was working. He winked his eye as he made his chest jump. I knew right then, and there I needed to get out of here.

"Thanks for the invite, but I have got to go." I tried to walk off the balcony and into the room, but he stopped me. He damn near had me cornered on the balcony.

"You lying. I'm sorry if I made you uncomfortable. I have that type of effect on women. I won't bite unless you want me to."

He was so close up in my face and in my personal space that his breath tickled my nose. I guess the liquor and weed got the best of me because I leaned in and started kissing him. When he slipped his tongue into my mouth, my panties magically slipped off.

"No Sheik! People will see us." He had me bent over outside of the balcony ready to go in.

"That's exactly what I want. Trust me, Yoka. I got you."

All logic went out the door as he slipped his dick inside of me. I bit down on my bottom lip as he touched my inner soul with each stroke. I gripped the railing as I braced myself for his impact. He was thrusting in and out of me with so much intensity that I thought I might go right over the balcony. In that moment, I was in pure ecstasy. The fact that he was stranger or that we weren't even using protection didn't matter. At this point in my life, I guess any attention from any nigga was better than the attention I had got from Zuri. Without warning, Sheik picked me up, carried me into the room, and laid me down on the bed. There was something different in his eyes as he laid on top of me. What started off as straight fucking turned into a love-making session out of this world. This nigga was slanging cock, and I was taking every inch of it. After what seemed like hours of fucking, the last thing I remembered before falling asleep was him kissing my toes.

∼

THE SOUND of someone banging on the hotel door caused me to jump up out my sleep. I could tell Sheik was in shock too because he was sitting up half sleep trying to see what was going on.

"Open this door, Sheikem!"

"Who the fuck is that?"

"Fuckkkk! That's my wife."

"Your wife!"

"Look just be cool. I'll explain later." He jumped up, threw on clothes, and went outside. Yelling arguing could be heard clear as day.

I was mad as fuck at myself for fucking this nigga and not asking any questions. I jumped up from the bed and went in search of my dress. My shit was on the damn balcony soaking wet. Since I didn't have shit, I looked for his suitcases and went in search of a shirt. When I opened his luggage, I grabbed the first shirt I saw and put it own. Once I removed it, I wish I hadn't. This nigga had clothes covering bricks. This nigga was married and a fucking drug dealer. Let me get the hell out of here.

Once I could no longer hear arguing I quickly got the fuck out of dodge. I felt like I was doing the walk of shame as I walked through the parking lot to get to my car. I felt relieved as I sat in my driver's seat.

"You thought you could keep running from a nigga, huh?" My eyes widened looking at Zuri in my backseat. Before I could say anything, he punched me hard as fuck in the back of my head making me lose consciousness.

6

AZADA

Hurt was an understatement as I sat across from Sheik. In my heart, I knew he was with another bitch. I could feel it in my soul that he had been with someone else. He wouldn't even let me into the hotel room. When he walked out of the room, he looked off to me. The worse part of it was that I could smell the bitch all over him. I don't even know why I'm acting surprised at the shit. This ain't nothing new he's getting bolder with the shit, and that's what bothers me. I'm just at my wit's end with the bullshit. We've been together for what seems like forever, but at the same time, that nigga doesn't love me anymore. I just wish I knew what I had done to make him turn so cold.

"You just gone sit here and not say shit, nigga?" Sheik sat cutting his steak and eating like it was nothing.

"I honestly don't know what the fuck to tell you. It's your fault. You came to my fucking room. You know I'm down here doing business. The last thing on my motherfucking mind is a bitch. If memory serves me right, I tried to get you to bring your ass with me, but you were more interested in going shopping in New York with your hoe ass friends!" He hit the table, causing all of the other patrons to turn around and look. I was so embarrassed that tears welled up in my eyes.

"I know that Sheik, and I'm sorry. When I got there, I turned around and came right back because I felt like shit. Just be honest with me. Were you with another woman?" My heart raced as I waited for him to answer. A part of me wanted the truth, but the other part of me was scared to know.

"Yeah, I was. She was here to give me what I needed when my wife wasn't. Go home, Azada." My heart was crushed. I sat with my head hung low as the tears flowed. He was so damn cold-hearted and nonchalant.

"Are you coming home tonight?" Grabbing a napkin from the table, I wiped the tears from eyes.

"Nah! I'll be there first thing tomorrow though. We'll continue this conversation then." He kissed me on the forehead and walked away like it was nothing. I felt more like a bitch that he had fucked and bought lunch for, not the woman who carried his last name. This shit hurts so bad, and I don't wish it on my worse enemy.

I drove around aimlessly crying and lost as to what the fuck my next move would be. I wasn't a bad wife. I just became content with hanging out with my friends, shopping, and keeping up appearances. In the midst of that, I lost the connection with my husband. The last thing I want to do is lose him to another bitch. Then again who am I kidding. It looks like I've lost him already.

I sat outside of my mother's house almost too afraid to knock on the door. It had been so long since I had talked to her. She had been locked up for check fraud. My momma was a known card cracker and master manipulator. If I was going to be with Sheik, I had to cut ties with her or eventually he would become the mark he was initially supposed to be.

My mother had taught me the art of deceit from an early age. There was no one that I couldn't get over on. Shay-Shay had taught me well. The only thing about doing that shit was that I hurt a lot of people by stealing their identities and emptying their bank accounts. When I met Sheik, I no longer wanted that life. My momma had been fucking with this nigga Trick, and he wanted us to set him up and rob him. Instead of her doing it, she put me on him. My first night with him was magical. That nigga wifed me up, and I never looked back. He was too genuine and free hearted. I just couldn't bring myself to take anything from him. To this day, he has no idea that I was really trying to set him up on our first date.

Instead of getting out of my car and going inside, I decided just to head home. I needed to prepare myself for when my husband came home. I wasn't giving up on my marriage when it definitely deserved a fighting chance. I just hope Sheik still wants this. Lord knows I don't know what I'm going to do if he decides he wants out.

IT HAD BEEN A WEEK, and Sheik still hadn't come home nor had he answered the phone for me. I guess it was clear where we were as a couple. My ass had been crying like crazy. That sadness was starting to turn into anger, and that wasn't like me. At this point, I didn't know what to do. My mind was all over the place. I didn't know if the nigga was dead, in jail, or had left my dumb ass. The sound of someone banging on my door made me jump up out of bed and rush downstairs. When I opened the door, I wished that I hadn't.

"Nice to see you too, daughter?" I rolled my eyes looking at my mother.

"How did you get my address?"

"I saw Keena at the mall yesterday, and she told me. I've been looking for you, Muffin. Damn, you done married this rich nigga and said fuck your OG, huh?"

"It wasn't like that, Ma."

"That's exactly how it was? Fuck all that though. I'm just happy you're okay. Now show me around this fortress you call a house."

"Don't steal shit out my house, Momma. I'm so fucking serious." Besides her being a damn card cracker, her ass is a certified kleptomaniac.

"Girl Bye. I'm delivert. I'm no longer a thief, Muffin. Momma done gave her life to the Lord."

I shook my head at her because that was nothing but code for telling me that she is stealing from nice church folks. My momma ain't got no chill. It doesn't matter who you are. If you have something she wants, she's going to take it.

"Whatever! You just better not steal shit out my house."

"Anyway? This shit is boss as fuck!" she yelled as I showed her around the house. The sound of the alarm beeping made me run to the top of the stairs to see Sheik coming in the house.

"Who's piece of shit is that in my driveway?"

"That would be my piece of shit. I take it you're the infamous Sheik who has my daughter acting as if I don't exist." My heart raced listening to my mother say that shit to him.

"Nah, I think that would have to do with her upbringing. Come here, Azada. Let me talk to you!"

"I should have robbed that motherfucker!" she said under her breath were only I could hear her. I immediately gave her a look telling her to shut the fuck up. The last thing I needed was for him to hear the shit she had said.

"Stop it! I'll be right back."

As I headed down the stairs, my mind raced wondering what the hell he wanted. The nigga had a mean mug and a stern ass voice. I knew without a doubt this shit wouldn't be good. When I walked into his office, he was screwing a silencer on a gun.

"Should I kill her now or later?"

"Huh?"

"Don't huh me, Azada! Your momma is a snake ass bitch, and I know she sent you to play me in the beginning, but you fell for the dick and riches instead. Get that bitch out my shit!"

"That's my momma tho! I haven't seen her in so long. She just got out. Why are you making me choose?"

"Bitch, you been chose me when you cut her off. Don't stand right here like you love her card cracking ass. I'm telling you right now. I'm going to murk you and her if I even think it's some bullshit in the air.

She ain't popped up out if the blue for nothing." Sheik had lost his mind with the shit he was saying.

"Who is the bitch that got you feeling like you can handle me like this? Apparently, you're feeling her because you have never came at me like this. If it's over with us, let me know. I'm not trying to keep your disrespectful ass if you're not trying to be kept." He just started laughing like something was funny, and I definitely didn't see shit funny at the moment.

"I'm not the type of nigga that's kept. In case you forgot, I do all the keeping. Honestly, this shit's been over. The moment you got comfortable and thought you didn't have to act like a wife this shit was doomed. You're a grown ass woman who would rather shop than cook. You would rather hire a cleaning crew instead of cleaning your own fucking house. Keep it real with yourself, Azada. After three years, you haven't given me a seed, and that's because I never nut in your ass. Wife or not, my child will never have a drunk for a mother. Get your shit together if you want your marriage to work. You've been here, so I feel like you at least deserve a chance, but after this, I'm done. I don't want to hear shit about you trying. Trying and doing is two different things. Humble yourself and appreciate the fact you rock my last name cause its bitches out here who dying to do that shit."

He walked out of the office and seconds later, I heard the front door slam. I couldn't believe the shit he had said. I guess it's true when they say the truth hurts because a bitch was hurt. I would be lying if I said I didn't love him because I loved the fuck out of him, but in my heart, I knew he was fucking somebody else. I could either save my marriage or fold. The funny thing about that is I've never been the type of bitch to fold. I'll fight for my marriage before I let another bitch have my husband. The sound of my mother laughing from behind me made me quickly wipe my face before turning around.

"What's so funny?"

"You standing here crying over a nigga who obviously doesn't love or respect you. Get your shit and leave now. I heard every word that nigga spat. This shit is over, Muffin. Hit his safe and let's bounce."

"I can't do that. I love him, Ma. I can't just walk out and lose him to another bitch."

"You already lost him to another bitch. Don't play yourself. I taught you better than to let a nigga treat you like that. At the same time, I loved the fuck out of your daddy, so I know how you feel. Fight for your marriage if you feel there's a chance. You know where to find me if shit don't work out." My mother kissed me on the forehead and left.

I could have robbed Sheik blind, but the real bitch in me couldn't bring myself to do it. That nigga had taken care of me, so I didn't see a reason for me to do snake shit like that. In the meantime, I would work on me as a woman. If he wanted a better wife, then that's what he was going to get.

SEVEN

I was going out of my mind with worry. Damn near to the point where I felt like I was going to lose my mind. It had been almost two weeks, and no one had heard or seen Yoka. Her mother had reported her missing and everything. This was so not like her. Something was wrong. I could feel it in my heart and soul that she wasn't okay. For some reason, I felt like Zu had something to do with her disappearance. The police had questioned him, and he said he hadn't seen or heard from her since she left him. His psycho ass was so good he had the police thinking that she wasn't in danger, but that she had just run away from their relationship. Yoka's mother had even put missing flyers up all over Miami and Georgia in the hopes someone would remember her.

The hardest part for me is the fact that the last time we spoke, we were arguing. My dumb ass was so wrapped up in proving a point to Hussein that I wasn't a good friend to her, and she was actually there with me. If something has happened to her, I'll never forgive myself. This thing with Yoka missing has me looking at shit differently and definitely saying fuck Hussein. It was like as I sat my dumb ass there watching him with his wife, a light bulb went off in my head, letting me know I needed to leave that man alone.

As I drove home that day from the party, I wondered how other women felt who managed to fall in love with a married man. The shit is pure torture on the heart and soul. I wouldn't wish this shit on my worst enemy. I keep wondering how I allowed myself to fall in love with him. Then I remember it was his brolic stature, big dick, head game, and his gift of the gab. The nigga could talk a bitch clean up out her panties. Besides that, he was very smart and charming. The thing I loved most about him was that we could lie in bed and talk for hours about everything. It was the little things that made me love him. At the same time, the love I have for Hussein is killing me. That shit is unhealthy. I'm just glad he hasn't been calling or texting me. It makes this shit much easier.

Pulling out my phone, I called Yoka in the hopes that she would pick up. My heart raced with each ring. Once it went to voicemail, tears welled up in my eyes. This couldn't be life. I needed to find out what the hell happened to my friend. Lord knows the police was not trying to find her.

~

I TREMBLED with fear as I took my gun off safety. My ass was in position behind my bedroom door ready to shoot whoever was coming in my house. At first, I thought I was losing my mind thinking that someone was jiggling my doorknob. I was living in a new house, and no one knew my damn address, so I was convinced a bitch was getting ready to die.

"Seven, where the fuck you at?" I shook my head and stepped from behind the bedroom door.

"What the hell are you doing here?"

"Don't ask me no questions! Fuck you doing moving and not telling a nigga?"

"Go home, Hussein!"

"I am home. Fuck you mean." I placed the safety back on my gun and placed it back underneath my pillow. I went from scared to irritated in a matter of seconds. I should have known this nigga wasn't going to just go away that easy.

"I'm not in the mood, Hussein. Just go ahead home to your wife and let her deal with your shit. I'm done. Stop playing with me, Hussein. I'm not in my right state of mind. My best friend is missing, and the man I love is married."

I didn't even mean to shed tears, but the shit with Yoka had got the best of me, not to mention his ass standing in front of me looking a whole meal. I plopped down on my bed and buried my face in my hands. I guess all of the emotions that were built up inside of me came out all at once.

"Just calm down. What you mean your friend missing?"

"My friend Yoka is missing. No one has seen or heard from her since that night of the party. This shit is all my fault. Had I just got up and left instead of trying to prove a point to you, shit would be different."

"Don't make me tell you to calm your ass down again. Look, let me get the word to some of my niggas in the streets. You look stressed the fuck out, and I don't like that. I know this shit between us been rough on you. I'm sorry for everything. The last thing I ever wanted to do was hurt you because you're such good people. I'm a nigga that wanted my cake and eat it too. I know that shit sounds fucked up, but you deserve the truth. A nigga wants Kimora and you, but obviously, it's not what you want, and I understand. Out of respect for you lil baby, I'll stand down. I'd rather have you as a friend than not have you at all. Get you some rest and stay by your phone. I'll be calling you when I get some information."

"Wait! I need to give you my number."

"I got it already. Stop moving and changing your phone number, it's a waste of money. I run this city. Nothing gets past me." He winked at me and walked out of my bedroom.

At this point, I couldn't even be mad at him. A bitch had to respect him for being trill. Him noticing this shit was hurting me only made me love him a little more. We women are crazy creatures. I blame the shit on Eve. She's been getting us in fucked up situations with niggas ever since she bit that damn apple. On a brighter note, I'm happy he's going to help with Yoka being missing. He and Sheik run this city, so I know he will find out something. In the meantime, I'll just continue praying that Yoka is safe and sound.

8

YOKA

I was losing my mind locked up in the basement of the house that I shared with Zuri. This nigga had kidnapped and driven me all the way back to Atlanta in his damn trunk. I was trying to understand what fucking day it was. It was so fucking dark in the basement that I couldn't tell night from day because it was so dark. All the screaming and hollering I had been doing was useless. When Zuri built the house, he had it soundproofed so no one could hear. I've prayed for God to get me out of this situation but it seems like he's not listening. I know my momma is freaking out because she hasn't heard from me. This nigga got a whole bitch with a baby. He needs to let me out this fucking basement and live his life. I guess I can be thankful that he's only been coming by to drop off food and water. When he brings the food in, he doesn't look me directly in my eyes or say a word to me. I'm just praying he keeps it this way. At the same time, it's only a matter time before he blows up. That's how his crazy ass is. One minute he's nice, and the next he's a fucking monster.

≈

THE SOUND of the basement door opening made me sit up on the couch. I had been sleeping more than anything so that I could pass the time away. When I was awake, my mind went into overdrive. I was starting to lose my mind, and I didn't like it.

"You left me for another nigga, huh!" he yelled as he threw pictures at me.

I swallowed hard because I knew this nigga was gone off that powder. That shit made him evil as fuck, and I usually caught the repercussions of his addiction. I looked at the pictures, and they were of Sheik and I talking at the gas station. I was trying to understand who would be following me in his camp that damn fast to get pictures of me. That had my mind boggled.

"I didn't leave you for anybody, Zu. I left you because of the way you treated me. You have a whole family that you chose over me. Let me go, and you go home to them!"

"Shut the fuck up! It was always your fucking mouth that got you fucked up." The impact of his hand knocked the wind out of me, but I refused to cry. My mouth pooled with blood, and I spit on the floor.

"That nigga got you feeling yourself, but I'm about to remind you who the fuck I am." I balled up to hide my face as he delivered blow after blow.

With each punch, I felt like I was going to die. His fists felt so powerful as he unleashed his rage on me. I could swear I felt my rib when he cracked it. Once he was done using me as a punched bag, he grabbed a thick orange extension cord and wrapped it around his hand a couple of times.

"Please, Zuri stop!"

"You gone stay here!"

"Yesssssss! Just please don't hit me with that cord!" I cried, begged, and pleaded, but he still beat me with it. With each hit, I felt like I was going to pass out from the pain.

"Bitch, you gone learn today!" He dropped the extension cord and pulled some scissors out of his pocket. I just knew he was about to stab me. Instead, he held my head down and cut all of my hair off. He was such a bitch ass nigga for this shit. Like what real man does shit like this?

"I bet that nigga or any other nigga won't want your baldheaded ass now! Go upstairs and do your fucking duty as a woman." He grabbed me by the throat and choked me until I almost passed out. Despite damn near coughing up a lung, I managed to make it up the basement stairs. Once I made it to the living room, I stopped in my tracks looking at a sleeping baby on the couch.

"Keep an eye on my little man while I make this run. I expect dinner to be done when I get back or I'm going to beat your ass again."

Zuri walked out of the door like it was nothing. I didn't understand why I was being punished like this. Somewhere in my life, I had to have disappointed God. That's the only excuse I can come up with.

For some strange reason, I was standing in the same place staring at the baby. It was like I couldn't move. The craziness inside caused me to have visions of smothering the little boy, but I wasn't that type of person to harm an innocent child. I knew I needed to get out of here, but this is only a test. Zuri is not gone. He's dying to catch me trying to escape so that he can punish me more. In order for me to survive this shit, I needed to beat him at his own game. As I walked to the kitchen, I passed the mirror on the wall and glanced at it. I cringed looking at my bruised, bloodied, and swollen face, not to mention the fact that my once beautiful hair was gone.

I quickly wiped my tears and headed upstairs to my old bathroom. Everything was just as I had left it. Zuri hadn't been living here. It had been weeks since I showered and all I wanted to do was scrub my skin. I smelled horrible to the point where I was gagging off of my own scent. I sat on the side of the tub and turned on the water for a hot bath.

"That's right soak that pussy. The night is just getting started." I looked up, and Zuri was leaning against the bathroom doorframe with a toothpick dangling from his mouth. This is typical Zu I knew he wasn't gone. He was just testing me.

"Why are you doing this to me?"

"Because you're a liar and a deceiver. You promised me that you would never leave me no matter what. I told your ass the only way you would ever leave is in a fucking body bag. I meant that shit. I'll kill your ass and make sure they never find your ass. As a matter of fact, let me show you something real quick."

He yanked me up and basically pulled me down the stairs. I held on to the banister to keep from falling. Swinging open the door to the garage he pushed me inside so hard that I fell on top of a blue tarp. I quickly jumped up when a piece of it fell open.

"Ahhhhhhhhh!" I screamed, looking at his baby momma Da'Loni's lifeless body.

"I killed her so that we can fix this shit. Plus, I caught her stealing from me. Now go get your son. You wanted a baby, and now you have one."

This was some shit that happened in Lifetime movies, not in the fucking hood. This can't be life. Just knowing he was capable of killing me, I know I had to move with precision if I was going to survive this shit. Walking back into the living room, I couldn't help but feel sorry for the baby. His mother was dead, and his father was a sadistic son of a bitch. What in the hell would make him think killing his baby momma would make me want his ass? This nigga has kidnapped me, beat my ass, and cut my hair off. All I want to do at this point is inflict the same pain on him that he has inflicted on me. Although I hated her for basically ruining my life and relationship, I feel sorry for her. No woman deserves this shit. Just seeing her dead body lets me know that he will kill me with no hesitation. He's walking around like the shit he's doing is normal, and it's not. Something is definitely wrong with this nigga, and I have every intention on getting the fuck away from him. I never dreamed that I would feel like he would actually kill me all of these years we were together. Seven always said that Zuri wasn't right in the head. In the back of my mind, I knew he was fucked up, but it's like when you're in love with someone you become blinded by who they really are. It's sad because they show you every day. Love is a powerful thing it makes all logic and judgment go out of the window. Had I faced those signs head on, I wouldn't be in this predicament now.

"I don't have an issue with putting a fucking bullet in your head. So, don't get any bright ideas and think you can run away from me. Get comfortable Ni'Yoka because I refuse to let you leave me again. Just so you know I'm going to kill that nigga you been down there in Miami fucking. Now take your ass upstairs and take a bath."

As I walked back of the stairs, I cried just thinking about Sheik. This shit was all his fault. If his wife hadn't shown up to the hotel room that day, I wouldn't be here. Then again if Zuri was coming for me, he was coming. I can't blame that on Sheik. At the same time, I'm so fucking angry at him for never divulging that he was indeed married. The shit made me feel even worse about judging Seven. I had basically placed myself in a predicament that I wanted no parts of. The sad part about it is Sheik had me digging him. I had never experienced anything like that before. I felt stupid as fuck hearing that girl bam on the door like that. Either way, there is no need for me to even give the man a second thought since from the looks of things I'll never see him again.

After soaking until the water was ice cold, I finally got out of the tub. All my belongings were still the way I left them. As I threw on some clothes and a bonnet on my head, I could hear the baby crying at the top of his lungs. I sat down on the bed for just a minute to take it all in.

"Yoka! Get the fuck up and get our son! Don't you ever let him cry like that, do you understand me?"

"Yes, Zuri. I understand."

I got up from the bed and found the baby in the nursery that I had put together in the hopes that we would have a baby. It hurt that we actually never got to that point. As I leaned over in the crib to pick him up, I noticed just how much he favored his mom. It's a shame he'll never have her here to see him grow up. I hated to even hold this baby, but I knew that taking care of him was the only way either of us would survive this shit. At that moment, I sucked it up and accepted the fact that this would now be my life. At least right now anyway because the first chance I get I'm getting the fuck out of dodge.

～

"WHEN WE WALK in this motherfucker you better be on your best behavior. I don't give a fuck what my sisters or OG say. You take that shit in stride."

Zuri and I were headed over to his mother's house for Thanksgiving dinner. I was sick as a dog and had been throwing up frequently. I was sick as a dog and scared as fuck because I knew this nigga had got me pregnant. He had been raping me all day and every day. I wasn't really tripping because I knew I would soon have a miscarriage. I simply can't hold babies to save my life. I hope like hell that it happens soon this time. Hopefully, God will forgive me for feeling that way because I'm ready to get this shit over with. I still couldn't believe he was actually taking me out of the house. I was dreading going over here because of the events that happened the last time we were over there.

"Okay, Zuri. You don't have to keep reminding me." I didn't even see his fist coming towards me until it was too late. He had hit me so hard that my head bounced off the window.

"Watch who the fuck you talking you. Wipe your mouth before you get blood all over the place with your dumb ass."

I caught the napkins he threw at me and quickly pressed it up against my aching mouth. For the rest of the ride, he talked to random women on the phone while I sat in the passenger seat praying for death. Shit was harder than I thought it would be. My mind drifted to my mother. I know she must be going crazy not knowing where I am. She has been the main reason why I haven't given up so far. Pulling up to Zuri's mother's house, I had no idea how I was about to be able to act normal. I'm sure they would be wondering where Da'Loni was, and why I was here with Zuri and his son acting as if I'm his mother.

"I thought you weren't coming, son." Ms. Zora pulled him into her embrace, but quickly let him go when she saw me standing behind him with the baby.

"Hey, Ms. Zora. Happy Thanksgiving."

"Hey, Yoka. This is surprising." She walked over to me and grabbed the baby out of my hand." She looked me up and down as she cradled the baby.

"Look, Ma. I need to make a run real quick before everybody gets here. Keep an eye on my baby." He came over, and tongue kissed me. I cringed, but I knew I had to play it off. This was another test, so I didn't take this as an opportunity to run.

"I got you, baby. You already know that."

I swallowed hard as she spoke because she looked at me with a devious look in her eyes. It was something I had never seen before coming from Ms. Zora. Zuri gave me a look with stern eyes before walking out of the door. For a couple of seconds, I stood in the foyer as Ms. Zora walked away.

"Ma! We're here." Zuri's sister Zoey yelled as she walked through the door with her four bad ass kids. She looked at me and started laughing as she shook her head.

"I'm in the kitchen. Come on back here. You too, Yoka." I walked into the kitchen, and Ms. Zora was sitting at the table smoking a cigarette.

"What the hell is wrong with you?" Zoey asked me.

"Shut the fuck up, Zoey! I got this." Ms. Zora banged on the table. That's when I noticed the missing person's flyer on the table. Tears formed in my eyes because I couldn't believe that was my face staring back at me.

"I'm saying, Ma. This girl got people out here thinking she's missing, but she's actually here with Zuri. That's so fucked up. Her momma's been on the news begging and pleading for her safe return, and she's been okay the entire time."

"Why, Ni'Yoka? How could you do that? To make matters worse, you're here with Zuri and the son he had on you. Does Da'Loni know about this shit?"

"Please, Ma. You know damn well Loni don't know. She doesn't play about her baby."

I closed my eyes and tried my best to hold my composure, but how could I. Just listening to these bitches let me know that they were dumber than what they thought I was.

"Da'Loni doesn't know because Zuri killed her. Do you actually think I'm here willingly? He kidnapped me from Florida and has held me hostage in our old house since then. Does this look like I'm here with him willingly?"

I pulled my wig off my head and removed my shirt to reveal all the black and blue marks that covered me. My breasts had bite marks all over from him forcing me to ride him while he bit me like a damn animal.

"Oh, my god, Yoka!" Ms. Zora jumped up and turned me around to look at my back.

"Zu did this to you?" Zoey said as she covered her mouth in shock.

"Please help me. He's been beating me if I breathe wrong. Zu killed Da'Loni and buried her in the backyard. You have got to let me out of here before he comes back and kills me."

"Here! Take my car and just drop it off somewhere."

"But how will you and the kids get around."

"Don't worry about that. Just get the fuck out of here before his nutty ass comes back."

"I'm so sorry, Yoka. I didn't know." Ms. Zora said. I heard her but didn't have time to respond. I got the fuck out of dodge.

When I got far away, I stopped at a gas station and called my mom. I should have been calling the police, but at the moment all I wanted to do was let her know that I was okay.

~

IT HAD BEEN a month since I got away from Zuri. I had been with my mother since then and scared as fuck. Since I hadn't called the police, I was living in fear, not to mention I'm damn near three or four months pregnant and keeping it a secret. My mother was so engrossed in keeping me away from Zuri that she wasn't really looking at the way my body was changing. The big ass clothes I was wearing was helping me keep the pregnancy on the low.

I had never made it to four months, so this shit had me scared. There was no way I could give birth to Zuri's demon seed. My mother had been so good to me through all of this, but I wanted to go back to Florida.

"Are you sure about this, Yoka?" my mother asked as she drove me to the airport. I was ready to get the fuck out of dodge.

"Yes. I want to go back to Florida. I need to get the hell out of here, Ma. There is no telling when Zuri is coming, so I need to go. You can even come with me, Ma. I'm sorry I can't stay."

"I already talked with Ms. Zora. Zuri is long gone. He left that baby on her and everything."

"That doesn't mean shit, Ma! They will always take up for him. Zuri can be somewhere right now looking at us. I'm sorry, but I have to go."

"Okay baby. I love you. I'm just happy that you're okay. This incident has made me look at life so different. For so long I spent years trying to make you into the woman I wanted you to be. That made you rebel, and we lost time. When I thought that I would never see you again, I asked God to bring you back to me. All I wanted was a chance to make things right. Go to Florida and live your life. As long as you're okay, I'm okay."

We came to a red light, and she reached over to hug me. Before we could actually embrace, the sound of gunfire erupted, and that's the last thing I remembered.

9

SHEIK

F inding out that Yoka had been kidnapped had me feeling fucked up. She hadn't been seen or heard from since that night of the party. I was feeling kind of fucked up with the way she found out that I was married. A nigga just knew that she would still be in the room when I came back, but she was gone. That was the last time I had seen or heard from her. When Hussein came and told me about the shit that was going on I felt bad.

I was sitting and wracking my brain trying to figure out what had happened to Yoka. A nigga was so engrossed in her being missing that I paid no attention to the effort Azada was putting in. With Hussein and me coming up short on the streets, I knew this shit was deeper than a simple missing case. Since I couldn't find out anything the hood way, I decided to go back to the hotel and have the security run back the tapes from that day. It was then I watched in shock as she was abducted. It was obvious that whoever the nigga was had knocked her unconscious and placed her inside the trunk. That shit fucked me up because he basically drove out of the parking lot with her like it was nothing. A nigga felt like shit because I should have been there to protect her. I mean she did, after all, put her life on the line to let me know niggas was at my head, so she definitely deserved for me to look out for her. The police hadn't been doing shit, so I was going to make it my business to find out where the fuck she was at.

Seven kept talking about some nigga named Zu might have her, and I had my people in Atlanta looking into it. She might not be my woman, but I owe her my life for the shit she did for a nigga, not to mention feeling responsible for the shit. I know people would look at me wrong for saying this, but I would have rather woke up inside of her and not Azada banging on the damn door.

"CAN WE TALK?" Azada asked when I walked into our bedroom.

"Yeah. What's good?"

"Who is Ni'Yoka, and why are you looking for her?"

"She's a friend," I quickly answered and walked inside of the bathroom.

I prayed Azada didn't make a big deal out of this. She had been doing good at trying to fix shit, but I wasn't trying to discuss Ni'Yoka with her. The last thing I needed was for her to ask questions because I wasn't going to lie.

"Did you fuck her?"

"Yeah, I did."

"Fuck you, Sheik! I'm walking around this motherfucker doing everything in my power to make shit right, but you out here looking for some missing bitch that you fucked. I knew I should have just cut my losses and bowed out gracefully. I refused to allow your ass to make a fucking fool of me. Here it is I'm bussing my ass to cook dinner and spend time with you, but your ass won't even come home."

I looked at this crazy bitch ranting and raving. This was why I didn't want her to inquire about Yoka. I flamed up a blunt and looked at her like the crazy bitch she was. The last thing I want to do is hurt her feelings, but sometimes you have to put bitches in their place because they forget shit.

"Let's get some shit straight. The shit you've been doing is the shit a wife supposed to do. I'm not about to act like you're doing something spectacular. As far as you cutting losses and bowing out, you can beat your feet as far as I'm concerned.

"I should have listened to my momma. She was right when she said your ass was done with me. I was just too blind to see it. If it's over between us, then we can end it here. There doesn't have to be a messy divorce. I'll sign the papers with no hesitation. All I ask is for the house in Palm Beach, to keep my cars and all of my possessions that I've acquired during the marriage, and fifty thousand to go with the fifty thousand I have to start my life over."

"You got that. I'll call Don at the bank so that he can have that money for you. Do me a favor and listen to me. Don't let your snake ass momma trick you out your money or make you go back to your old ways. You're better than that. Just because we didn't make it, doesn't mean you don't deserve to be happy. You and I both know she ain't popped up out the blue for nothing. I'm telling you right now I will chop her up and feed her to my piranhas if she fucks with me."

I kissed Azada on the forehead and went into the bathroom to take a shower. It wasn't that I didn't love Azada I just wasn't in love with her anymore.

10

YOKA

For hours I had been sitting in my hospital room staring into space. I was trying to figure out how I was going to be able to go on without my mother. It was killing me because I knew Zuri was behind the shit. My ass was regretting not contacting the police about him kidnapping me. My mother didn't deserve to lose her life behind my bullshit. I have no idea how I'm going to live the rest of my life knowing that my mother is dead because of me. The police had talked to me, and there was nothing I could actually tell them. I didn't see anything or anyone. That added with the fact that one of the officers that were questioning me was cool with Zuri. There was no way I was saying shit about that nigga to him. For all I know, Zuri sent the nigga here. Hearing the monitoring beeping made me cringe. It measured my baby's heartbeat. I wanted to cry out in anger because I was still pregnant with Zuri's demon seed.

"I'm so happy you're okay?" Seven rushed inside of the room and wrapped her arms around me. I couldn't do anything but cry because I missed the fuck out of the crazy bitch.

"He killed her!"

"Shhhh! Stop crying everything is going to be okay. Here get dressed. We're getting out of here and going back to Florida."

"I can't. I have to give my mom a service."

"Don't worry about all that. Hussein and Sheik's got it covered. Come on. This hospital is not secure enough. There is no telling where that crazy ass Zuri is at."

"Why would Sheik and Hussein be handling my mother's funeral arrangements? They don't know her or me." I was side-eyeing the shit out of Seven because Sheik was on my list of niggas I wasn't fucking with.

"I don't have time right now to explain that. Get dressed Yoka so we can go."

"I'm pregnant. How can I raise a baby that has Zu's blood running through it? Seven, I don't want this baby." I didn't mean to break down and start crying about it, but I had become overwhelmed.

"Stop crying. All you ever wanted was to be a momma. Embrace that shit. Fuck it. I'll be the damn pappy. In the meantime bitch, let's ride. We can cry later at the crib." I laughed as I wiped my tears. Only Seven had the power to make me laugh while I was having a complete meltdown.

~

ABOUT AN HOUR later I was at Seven house resting in the guest bedroom. The gunshot wound I had sustained to my chest had me exhausted. It was a miracle that me or the baby survived. I guess I should be embracing the fact that I am still here, but how can I when my mother is dead?

"You should come and sit outside to get some fresh air."

"I'm good. These meds are kicking in, and all I want to do is sleep. I'll sit out there when I wake up."

"Good because I want to hear about what the fuck happened between you and Sheik. Both of y'all are tiptoeing around the topic, and I need to know. Bitch, you know I'm nosey as fuck."

I rolled over on her ass and tried dozing off. The last thing I want to relive is the greatest night of my life that turned into the worst morning of my life. I still can't believe that nigga is married.

~

"WAKE UP! Sheik is out here, and he wants to talk to you." Seven was shaking me roughly out of my sleep, and I was tempted to slap the fuck out of her.

"Tell him to go home to his wife because I don't feel like talking."

"Well, that's too bad because I have some shit I need to say and you don't have a choice but to listen."

I lifted my head and damn came all over the place. Sheik was standing in the doorway looking like a full-course meal. He was rocking an all black Polo jogging suit with construction Timbs. The nigga looked thugged out as fuck." Since he wanted to fuck with me, I decided to fuck with him.

"What will your wife say about this? You sure she won't be banging on the door looking for your ass." I rolled my eyes and turned my back to his ass.

"Excuse us for a minute, Seven."

"Nigga please, this is my damn house!"

"Aye, Seven! Let me holla at you for a minute!" Hussein yelled. That bitch jumped up quick. I shook my head. Hussein got her wrapped around his finger.

"Nigga, you lucky," she said as she walked out of the room.

"I know finding out that I was married was fucked up, and I apologize for that shit. I'm not about to stand here and feed you no bullshit. I'm not one of these niggas that go around lying about his relationship status. However, I am a nigga that don't feel the need to tell people my business off top, especially when it doesn't concern them. At that moment, I just wanted to have a nice night with you. Stop sitting here fronting like you didn't enjoy this dick. Lord, knows I enjoyed every inch of being up in that pussy. That's neither here nor there. I'm actually here to apologize. A nigga feels responsible for that shit happening to you. Had Azada not shown up I would have been the one kidnapping you. All I ask is that you accept my apology and allow me to give your mother a home going service on me." I continued to lay in silence, taking in everything that he was saying.

"It's not your fault. Zuri would have found me eventually. Had I known he was capable of all of this, I would have done something sooner when he was beating my ass if I breathed too loudly. I accept your apology, Sheik. You don't have to pay for my mother a fancy service. She never wanted a funeral service because she said she didn't want her enemies looking at her dead body. She wanted a private cremation and for her ashes to be emptied at sea."

"Done. I'll hit you up when I get everything together."

"Thanks, Sheik."

I wanted to be mad at him but how could I when he was genuinely apologizing, not to mention coming out of pocket to give my mother her last wishes. The least I could do was accept his token of apology.

"Don't mention it. Oh yeah, don't worry about that fuck nigga ever fucking with you again. I got my people on him. So, you can rest comfortably. If that nigga even touches the Florida state line, I'll know about it." Sheik didn't give me a chance to respond before he walked out of the room. Seconds later, Seven walked back inside of the room

"Bitch, that nigga's such a boss. Y'all need to make this shit official. It's obvious he's feeling you. Plus, he and his wife are no longer together. You better snatch that nigga up before another bitch does."

"I'm good. The last thing I need in my life is a man, not to mention the fact that I'm pregnant with another nigga baby. These niggas are not trying to be with a bitch that has kids already."

Seven sat quietly because she knew I was telling the truth.

IT HAD BEEN a month since the incident, and I was back at home for the first time. Being at Seven's house was cool, but I liked my own space. I hadn't heard from Sheik since the cremation services, and I was actually happy about that. My stomach had seemed to get a little big overnight, and I was embarrassed as fuck behind being pregnant by Zuri. He was still on the run, but Sheik had me feeling like I was safe as ever. We hadn't talked, but he had security detail sitting outside of my house. The crazy part about it is that Zuri is the last thing on my mind. I've come to grips with being pregnant with his child, and I've decided to love this baby. No matter what happens, I have every intention of doing what I have to do to be a great mother. God has given me everything I ever wanted in the form of a child, so it's only right I do right by this baby. Zuri has had enough power over me, and I refuse to give him any more of my power. This is my new life, and I plan to live it my way. After all, my mother wouldn't want me not living my life and being a good mother.

The sound of Sheik's voice coming from outside made me rushing to the door. I opened it and noticed that he was having a damn meeting outside my house with several men. They were all in a huddle, and I was embarrassed as hell. I just knew my neighbors were looking out of their windows at these damn thugs having what looked like a gang meeting.

"What are you doing?"

"Just checking the trap and making sure you're safe and secure."

I was blushing like crazy on the inside because I couldn't show it on the outside. My first night with him was amazing, and I just keep reliving that shit. It's a shame I'll never get that back.

"I'm good. Now can you please break that up before my neighbors call the police?"

"I got you. Max is going to call your phone in about an hour so that you can feed that little one." He winked at me and hopped in his car, speeding off quickly.

I looked down and realized my robe had opened up. My small baby bump was showing. I didn't even know how to feel about that because I had plans on hiding this shit from him for as long as I could. Since the cat is out of the bag, I'm sure he'll disappear anyway. Not that he had a reason to stay, but him looking out for me had made me become more comfortable.

I stood in front of my floor length mirror staring at the scars that covered my body, not to mention my stomach. I wondered how long it would be before I was huge and wobbling around. The thought of bringing a life into the world to raise alone was scary as fuck. However, I have every intention of doing just that.

~

"You scared the shit out of me!" I said out of breath. Sheik was sitting at the foot of my bed.

"I was wondering how long your ass was going to be sleep. You sleep too hard, my love. Come on get dressed. I have something I want to show you." I stared at him irritated as fuck. For one I was tired as fuck, and he had basically broken into my damn house.

"Look, Sheik. I appreciate all of this you're doing for me, but you've done enough. As you know, I'm with child, and the last thing I want to do is burden you with another man's baby. Please leave and let me go to sleep."

"Get dressed! I'll be outside." He walked out of my bedroom like I hadn't said shit and that made me even more irritated.

The sound of him bumping Moneybag Yo loud as fuck made me jump up. It was obvious he wasn't going anywhere. I made sure to take my sweet time getting dressed.

After about an hour or so I was dressed and ready to go wherever he was taking me to. I hoped he wasn't trying to fuck or nothing like that. The last thing on my mind was having sex with his married ass. The last thing I needed to be was dick silly behind his ass. Seven is dick silly enough for the both of us.

"It took you long enough. I thought I was going to have to come inside and drag you out."

"Where are you taking me, Sheik? I don't feel too good, and I really just want to lay down."

"I got you. Lean your seat back and rest."

He cut the music up and sped off like he was crazy. I immediately put on my seatbelt before he killed my ass driving crazy and shit. As he drove vibing to the music, I found myself stealing glances at him. He was sexy as fuck. I could tell the nigga was a heartbreaker. I'm glad his wife showed up when she did. That nigga got that voodoo dick that would have a bitch walking around on her head. I'm good on that shit. I closed my eyes and tried dozing off, but it was hard as hell when he was playing loud ass music. I decided just to sit up and enjoy the scenery. There was something about the beautiful water and palm trees in Florida. It was a world away from the streets of Atlanta.

"These houses are so dope. This has to be where the rich folks reside. Are you sure we still in West Palm Beach?" I looked on in amazement at the many houses. Not to mention the upscale shops that adorned the side streets. I needed to hurry up and get my store popping because a bitch could definitely live out here.

"This is Palm Beach Island, and yes this is where the rich folks live."

I heard Sheik talking, but I was too busy looking at the scenery. When he stopped the car that's when he got my attention. He reached out of the driver side window and placed his index finger on a pad, and a huge gold gate opened up.

"This is your house?"

"Yeah. This is one of them. Get out so I can show you around." I was baffled as to why he wanted to show me around this damn mini-mansion. I side eyed his ass the entire walk up to the door. When we walked inside, everything was covered up. This might be one of his homes, but it was obvious he didn't stay here.

"What exactly are you showing me because this house doesn't look like it's been lived in for some time. Please explain to me why you got me out of my comfortable ass bed to look at these damn sheets."

"Because the beds here are much more comfortable. Here these are yours." He dropped some keys and paperwork in my hand. I opened the papers, and it was the deed to the house with my name on it.

"Oh no! Here Sheik, this is too much. You've done enough for me. I can't take nothing like this from you. It's not right. Here get this shit and take me back to my house." This nigga was tripping giving me a damn house.

"Look, this is just a token of my appreciation. You saved my life. Had you never risked your life I wouldn't be here. Them niggas had a whole hit out on my ass. I'm forever indebted to you. Plus, you need a better place to live before you give birth. Don't even think about giving me that shit back. Get comfortable. Seven is on her way to help you get the place in order. Max will be over with your things."

"Wait a minute, Sheik. I can't just leave my condo like that."

"Just trust me. I got you okay. It ain't safe for you living over there. If you think that nigga don't know where you stay your ass crazy. Just chill and stay here."

"Don't think I'm fucking you again."

"It's cool, ma. I get pussy on a regular. Plus, I already had you." He winked his eye and walked out the door.

I didn't know if I should have been turned on by his cockiness or pissed off from the disrespect. Either way, it looked like I was staying. Him mentioning Zuri knowing where I stayed at made me quickly put my pride away.

"I don't know what the fuck you did to that nigga, but it must have been damn good. He gave you a fucking house!" Seven screamed as we put dishes away.

"I told your ass I tried to give it back. What the fuck was I supposed to do? The nigga put my name on the deed."

"Bitch, you better not try to give this shit back no more. That would have been stupid ass fuck. I wish Hussein would give me a fucking house." That was the first time I heard her speak that nigga name and not sound hurt. Sis was letting that hurt go.

"Speaking of Hussein what's up with you and him."

"Shit. We cool. We've decided not to fuck around anymore for the sake of our friendship. That nigga ain't trying to leave his wife, and I'm not trying to be a side bitch anymore. I love him, but I love me more. Fuck all that though. Let's talk about you and that nigga Sheik. What's going on over here? I feel like you holding back on your girl."

"There is nothing between him and me. We had sex, and his wife came banging on the damn hotel door the next morning. He wasn't truthful about being married. That bitch was banging on the door and my ass had to hide on the balcony naked as fuck. Not to mention when I was looking for some shit to throw on, the nigga had bricks for days in his suitcase. To put the icing on the cake, my ass ended up getting kidnapped that day. All of that shit is a sign for me not to fuck with Sheik like that. I just hope and pray his wife don't bring no shit to this doorstep."

Just thinking about that made me uneasy as hell. I'm not in no condition to be fighting no bitch over they nigga. Yeah, I know he said they're separated, but I really can't believe shit he says in regards to his wife.

"Well, I can assure you he was out in these streets trying his best to find you. He felt bad as hell. He and Hussein showed me a different side of them when they were out doing the footwork to help me find you. Don't be too hard on him."

I was listening to Seven, and it made me feel good knowing that he was actually out and about looking for me. Sheik is one of those guys that has a heart of gold but is also the typical nigga. He's just going to be who he is. At the same time, I can't take that away from him because his good heart definitely trumps his whorish ways.

As I sat more dishes inside the cabinet, I quickly grabbed my stomach. For the first time, I felt the baby kick. The feeling was indescribable. It had made my heart flutter. I remember being pregnant and wanting to experience this, but I could never hold the baby long enough. At this point, I'm just ready to give birth. This feeling has me more than ready to meet my prince or princess.

11

SEVEN

I was so happy for Yoka but worried at the same time. Zuri needed to hurry up and be caught because I was uneasy with his ass loose. At the same time, I was also confident that Sheik would get his ass. With Yoka needing help with the baby, I decided to surprise her with a nursery. It seems like time is flying and before we know it the baby will be here. She's now five months, and her belly is getting bigger by the minute. I'm so happy that her mindset about this is in a more positive place. I could tell being pregnant by Zuri was taking a toll on her when she first made it back to Florida. She's now embracing the situation and the happiest I've seen her in a long time. Besides having me around for support, she has Sheik, and I think he's the real reason why she's in a much better place. Yoka can deny it all she wants to, but I think she loves Sheik. Her pride just won't let her admit it.

After a long day at work and shopping, I decided to go out and have a drink. It had been a minute since I enjoyed myself. Life was good, and things were working out in my favor. A nice stiff drink was definitely what a bitch needed.

As soon as I walked inside of Club Heaven, I wanted to walk back out. Hussein's wife Kimora and her crew were throwing daggers as soon as they saw me. I shook my head and grabbed me a seat at the bar. I wasn't thinking about them whack ass bitches. There was no need for me to even feed into the bullshit. Hussein and I weren't fucking around anymore. She should be happy I'm not riding his face anymore and making her taste it. The bitch better leave me the fuck alone.

"Here you go. The beautiful lady over there sent it." I looked at the waitress like she was crazy as she pointed in Kimora's direction.

This bitch and her crew held their glasses high and laughed. I laughed right with their ass as I popped open the bottle of Ace of Spades she had sent over. What did she think I was going to be offended? Hell no. If the bitch wants to show out and make herself look foolish, I'll be a fool with her ass. Kimora got to be the dumbest bitch in the world sending over an expensive ass bottle of champagne to me. Behind every dumb bitch is a bunch of other dumb bitches cheering her on. Kimora needed to reevaluate the bitches she was sitting with. They think the shit cute, but real friends would have told her to keep her money and keep the shit gangsta. That's why I fucks with Yoka. She told me when I was embarrassing myself. My dumb ass chose not to listen.

After a couple of glasses of champagne, I was feeling decent. I knew it was time for me to head home. As I walked out of the club and towards the parking lot, I didn't even notice Kimora and her crew behind me. I was regretting leaving my gun in the glove compartment. Before I could make it to my car, these bitches were swinging and throwing punches. I swear I was trying my best not to fall on the ground, but these hoes had me faded. I managed to keep my footing but lost it when one of the bitches sprayed mace in my face. That shit blinded me, and before I knew it, I was on the ground balled up trying to cover my face. I swear if it was the last thing I did I was getting that bitch back. Hussein might as well get ready. He could get it too if he thought I was going to let this shit ride.

~

IT HAD BEEN two weeks since I was jumped and my eyes had finally started to heal. Them bitches had got me good. Both of my eyes were black and bloodshot, not to mention I had a sprained wrist and ankle. I was more pissed off about missing work more than anything. I didn't have any more vacation days, so I missed pay. Hussein was definitely going to pay my bills for the motherfucking month. I still hadn't called or said anything to him about his wife and her friends jumping me. Apparently, the bitch hadn't said shit either because I know for a fact Hussein would have at least reached out to me. My ass didn't tell Yoka either because she would probably be out trying to fight bitches. I couldn't have that. I lied to her ass and told her my phone was broke so we couldn't Facetime.

It had been a minute since I smoked a blunt, but I made sure to face one before knocking on Hussein and Kimora's door. I knew both of them were inside because their cars were in the driveway. I was happy I remembered their gate code to get inside their subdivision.

I was banging and kicking on their door bright and early in the morning. I didn't give a fuck if I woke up the entire neighborhood. A bitch was not leaving until me and that hoe scrapped head the fuck up. I never needed a weapon to fight any bitch. My father taught me how to box at an early stage, so it was no pressure to knock a bitch the fuck out.

"Kimoraaa! Bring ya bitch ass outside." I started kicking on the door hard as fuck.

"Fuck is you doing here, Seven?" Hussein yelled as he opened the door.

"I didn't come here to see you. Tell your wife to come outside and catch this fade.

"Fuck you mean catch this fade!"

"I'm not about to answer no fucking questions. Ask yo bitch why I'm here to whoop her ass. If she doesn't come out, I'm coming inside to fuck her up." I tried pushing past him, but he blocked me.

"Move, Hussein! You wife and her fuckin' friends jumped on me, and I'm about to beat that bitch ass!"

"Let her go, Hussein!" Kimora yelled from behind him, and that's when I noticed she had a gun. This bitch was such a fucking coward. I couldn't even take this hoe serious right now.

"Put that shit down, Kimora!"

"Hell nah! I'm not putting shit down. I should shoot that bitch for trespassing any motherfucking way. As a matter of fact, stay right there. I got something for you, bitch!"

"Girl, put the fucking gun down so I can beat your ass!" She was pissing me off doing everything to keep from fighting. Scary ass bitch.

"Seven, just leave and let me handle this shit!"

"Hell nah! Fuck that. The bitch was so tough with her friends when they jumped on me. Just let us fight head up."

I was getting angrier and angrier and was at the point where I wanted to fight him. He didn't know about the shit, but I didn't care. Right now, he was looking like a fucking enemy in my eyes. Before either of us could say anything, the police had pulled up full force.

"Here she is, officer. This is private property, and I want her arrested!" I shook my head at this police ass bitch.

"Everything is fine, officer. I have it under control." Hussein was trying to talk to the officer, but Kimora wasn't having that shit.

"No, he doesn't. This is my husband's mistress, and she tried to assault me. I want to press charges!"

"This is the rat bitch you wifed up!"

"You're under arrest, ma'am! Turn around." I shook my head as the police placed the cuffs on me.

The entire time Kimora was laughing and smiling like some shit was funny. Hussein looked heated because he hated the police. I could tell he was embarrassed at the way Kimora was behaving too. If I were him, I would be reevaluating her position. I know for a fact he has all types of shit in that house, but because she was so pressed about me, she didn't even consider the consequences that her husband could suffer behind her actions. That bitch thought she was doing something, but she wasn't because I was still beating her ass. Hussein can get it too if he tries to step in and stop me. Sitting in the back of the patrol car had me thinking about my foolish ass move. I should have just caught the bitch in the streets instead of going to their house.

~

"It took you long enough. Bring your ass on. This baby is sitting on my damn bladder."

"What the hell you doing here, Yoka?"

"Hussein sent me to bond your crazy ass out. Why the hell are you going to that man's house trying to fight his damn wife? I thought you were over his ass."

"I am over his ass. It's his wife who keeps fucking with me. About two weeks ago, the bitch and her friends jumped on me. That's why I went to their house to get that bitch back."

"Wait a minute. What the fuck you mean two weeks ago?"

"Look, don't go all crazy. I kept the shit to myself because I knew you were going to want to fight. Them bitches got me good too. I swear to God I want to beat that bitch ass so bad." I had become so angry that I was on the verge of shedding tears. That's how fucking mad I was.

"What the fuck did Hussein do?"

"He didn't do shit because he didn't know. I'm not mad at him. I just want to fuck that bitch up for the shit she pulled. My fucking eyes were black and swollen shut. I have got to get that bitch back."

"I'm so fuckin' mad you didn't tell me. Wait until I have this baby. I swear to God we gone get that bitch." Seeing Yoka heated had me laughing hard as hell. She had no problem with fucking a bitch up.

"Calm down, killa." I couldn't help but laugh at her ass. She was seriously mad as fuck.

"Don't tell me to calm down. I'm so mad for not being there with you, not to mention the fact that you didn't even tell me about the shit."

"Like I said I just didn't want to have you all worried. Stop all that yelling upsetting the baby. I'm good, so don't worry." As we drove off from the jail, I remembered my fucking car was still parked at Hussein's house.

"Fuckkkkk!" I yelled as I hit the dashboard.

"What's wrong with you?"

"My car is still at Hussein house. I know that bitch tore my shit up."

"Calm down. It's parked outside your house. Hussein had Max drive it over there. Speaking of Hussein, he's at your house waiting on you to get there." I shook my head in irritation, but the last thing I wanted was to be bothered with Hussein. I actually didn't want to be bothered.

"Take me to your house. I'm not going home. Don't answer your phone when he calls either. He can take his ass home to his rat ass wife."

Hussein hadn't done shit to me, but I was hating him at the moment. In a way a was feeling all this shit was his fault, but in my heart, I knew it wasn't. As we continued towards Yoka's house, I realized just how physically and mentally tired the day's events had made me. All I wanted was to get some sleep and forget about the fact that I had just gotten my ass out of jail.

12

HUSSEIN SHAKUR

I had been trying my best not to spazz out on Kimora. She was walking around like she hadn't done shit. It pissed me off because the shit her and her crew had pulled was whack as fuck. The shit had me looking at her sideways because she walked around me for two whole weeks acting like nothing happened. I'm even more fucked up behind Seven not coming to me and telling me what the fuck had happened. I would have handled Kimora accordingly.

I wished Seven wouldn't have just popped up at the crib because the last thing I wanted her to do was to go to jail behind some bull-shit. The fact that Kimora called the police fucked me up. She knows how much I hate them motherfuckers, not to mention I got guns and ammunition in the fucking house. All I needed was to give them people a reason, and they would have searched my shit, and both of us would have been going to jail. Her dumb ass was acting on impulse and forgetting that both of us are on parole.

As a matter of fact, it's obvious she doesn't give a fuck, especially since she's out in the street fighting like a ghetto ass hood rat. Just thinking of her out in the streets with them ghetto ass bitches, lets me know she's done a backwards spiral. Back when we first met, she was loud and ghetto as fuck. I told her ass off top don't no nigga want a bitch that's unladylike, and if she wanted to fuck with me, she was going to have to fix that shit. I had an image to uphold, and I couldn't have my main bitch making me look bad.

At the same time, I loved how trained to go she was. Kimora had no issue with setting shit off for a nigga or trafficking bricks across state lines. That shit was like a gift and a curse for a nigga like me. I was in the streets heavier then and in my mind a Bonnie is what I needed. Years later and several stints in prison for both of us makes me want different. Kimora has been riding with me and been loyal to a nigga. However, that loyalty has become a burden because I'm no longer in the mood for a ride a die bitch next to me in the streets. I want a wife that stays home and make shit comfortable for a nigga after a long day of trapping.

I waited at Seven's house for hours, but her ass never came. I already knew she was pissed and not coming home because I was there. Sheik had already told me her ass was hiding out at Yoka's with her. It's cool for now. I'll give her ass some space, but eventually, she will have to listen to what the fuck I have to say. Kimora had been calling me like crazy, but I had been ignoring her ass. She had me so pissed off that I cut my phone off on her ass. Instead of me going home tonight, I'm taking my ass to my momma's crib. It's been a minute since I fucked with my OG anyway.

"WOULD YOU PLEASE CALL KIMORA? She keeps calling my phone using up my damn minutes," my mother said as I walked in the kitchen. She was sitting at the kitchen table watching the TV that we had mounted on the wall for her since that was her favorite place to be.

"What you mean minutes? I just got you an iPhone last month." This lady refuses to use updated shit. She's old school for real, and I hate it. Both Sheik and I go out of our way to buy her all of the latest shit for herself and her house, but she refuses to use it.

"Fuck that damn I-shit! Y'all pay all that money on them phones for nothing. I'm tired of that phone. That damn lady Sarah keeps talking to me, and it be pissing me off.

"It's Siri, Ma."

"Siri, Sarah, I don't give a fuck what the bitch name is. I keep telling y'all the government got them phones tapped. All of my years on this earth I never had a woman just talk to me out of the blue. Fuck that! I got warrants from back in the day. The last thing I need is to get knocked because Sarah wants to strike up a conversation I'm good." I just stared at her as she rolled her some tobacco up like a cigarette. Her government phone rang, and she ignored it.

"Why you not answering, Ma?"

"That's Kimora calling. I'm not answering shit. The only time she calls me is when y'all into it or when her ass is in jail. She nice as hell when she needs me for something, but when she doesn't, I'm invisible to her. That's fine by me because I told you a long time ago to leave her rowdy ass in them projects where you found her. Hand me a beer out the fridge. My show is getting ready to come on."

"Here. I'm about to go back here and lay it down. Don't answer for her or don't let her in here if she comes over. I just need a peace of mind."

"Well, you need to go to your own damn house and find peace. I like to walk around naked. How long you plan on being here anyway? Mr. Charlie likes to come over after he finishes delivering mail."

"Really, Ma?"

"Hell yeah! I'm old, not dead."

"I don't want to hear this. I'm getting out of here first thing in the morning. If I wake up and Mr. Charlie is in here, I'm going to beat his old ass." My mother bussed out laughing, but I didn't find shit funny. I was serious as fuck.

I wondered if Sheik knew Mr. Charlie and momma be fucking. His old ass has been the mailman for our hood for as long as I can remember. Just thinking about it makes me sick to my stomach. I went in the guest bedroom and laid it down. A nigga must have been tired as fuck because I was asleep before my head could hit the pillow good.

～

THE NEXT MORNING I sat outside Yoka's house. Seven was still avoiding me and acting like I was the one who had did something to her. Since she wanted to be petty with me, I decided to pop up on her ass. She don't have a choice but to holla at a nigga. It was a good thing I had an old key that my brother had given me when he still stayed on the property.

Both Yoka and Seven were knocked out sleep in the living room. They looked like they had a slumber party or some shit. Food boxes and chip bags were everywhere. I didn't mean to stop and stare at Seven sleeping. It's just that she looked so good even with slob coming out of her mouth. I walked over to the chaise where she was sleeping and moved the hair out of her face.

"What the hell? Nigga, you scared the shit out of me." Seven jumped up and got ready to swing, but I grabbed her hand.

"Calm your ass down. Let me holla at you." She snatched away from me and walked towards the back of the house. Of course, I followed her ass. She went into the bathroom and stopped in her tracks.

"If you don't want me to piss on your ass I suggest you move out the way."

"Sit down and piss. You acting like I ain't never saw that fat motherfucker before." She rolled her eyes and slammed the door in my face. That shit didn't faze me because I had all day. Either way, she was going to talk to me.

"I'm beating your wife's ass when I have this baby. Leave that key on the counter too. Breaking and entering is a felony, my nigga. Trespassers will be shot," Yoka said as she wobbled her ass past me.

She had got some spunk being around my brother. Speaking of him, he had me confused as fuck with the shit he was doing behind this girl. They aren't in a relationship, but she's being treated like a kept woman. That nigga ain't fooling me. He has some deeper feelings for Yoka then he cares to admit.

"You're still out here. I thought your ass got tired and left." Seven tried to brush past me, but I yanked her back.

"I know you mad but stop all this shit. I'm sorry about the shit that Kimora did. You know motherfucking well that shit would have been addressed accordingly had I known about the shit. All I'm asking is that you stop being mad at me."

I was definitely all up in her personal space. That shit made a nigga dick get hard because it had been a minute since I was in her presence. With us deciding to be friends, I made sure to keep my distance because I knew I couldn't control myself. Besides that, I didn't want to hurt her or play mind games with her. When you fuck with somebody the way I fuck with Seven, you have to move differently. She's someone who I would rather have in my life as at least a friend than not have her at all.

"Honestly, I'm not mad at you. You didn't do anything. I'm just super frustrated. Like every time I think about them bitches jumping me, I want to explode. They fucked my eyes up. I couldn't even go to work for two weeks. My bills and shit are going to be behind because of this."

"Look, stop worrying. I got you. I'll pay your bills for the next six months. Don't trip." Before I knew it, I grabbed her chin and kissed her on the lips. She quickly stopped me and moved away from me. I moved closer to her, but she blocked me.

"Stop it, Hussein! This is the reason all of this is going on in the first place. Had I never fucked you, your wife wouldn't have fought me. In a way, I can't be mad at her, but the bitch should have fought me head up. I can't keep investing my heart into a man whose heart belongs to another woman. That shit be hurting me because I love you. However, I have to love you from a distance in order to take care of my own heart. Go home to your wife." She walked away from me and went inside one of the bedrooms.

I stood there for a minute, but I had to walk away when I hear her crying. That killed me because I've been trying to avoid causing her any hurt or pain. For this reason, it's better that I do steer clear of her.

The drive home was filled with silence. My thoughts were

consumed with Seven and Kimora. Both of these women had the potential to drive me crazy as hell. The mood I was in made me want to head to the bar and drink. However, it was too fucking early. Plus, there was only so long I could go on ignoring Kimora. The shit she pulled had to be addressed. I just hoped and prayed she didn't make me lay hands on her ass. It had been years since I fucked her up, and I vowed to never put my hands on her again. Her mouth is reckless, and it will have you wanting to body her ass.

About an hour later, I pulled into the driveway. Before going in, I said a prayer and asked God to help with addressing this situation. I made sure to tell him to cover her in the blood because if she popped slick, I was going to fuck her up. As I put the key in the door, it swung open, and I knew then this shit wasn't going to go good. She had a blunt dangling from her mouth and a glass of wine in her hand. It wasn't even ten in the morning, and she was getting fucked up.

"Well, look at what the fuck the cat drug in?"

"I'm telling you right now to watch your fucking mouth, or I'm going to pop you in it. The way I'm feeling about the shit you pulled will make me snap. I advise you to go sleep that shit off and holla at me later."

"Nah, nigga! You're going to talk to me right now. Where have you been all night? I've been calling your phone, your momma's phone, and Sheik 's phone. Be a man about the shit. I know you were with that bitch because I smell her cheap ass perfume on you. That's why I don't regret beating that bitch ass. She knows that you're a married man and continues to fuck you."

I sat on the couch and flamed up a blunt. Kimora was making a fool out of herself, but I refused to stoop to her level.

"Actually, you didn't beat her ass. You and your friends jumped on her."

"Let me find out you taking up for that bitch!"

"It's not about me taking up for her. Right is right and wrong is wrong. For your information, I cut that shit off with her for the sake of our marriage. Maybe I should have kept fucking her since the street life is more important to you."

"Nigga, please! I've been in the streets since you met me. As a matter of fact, I've been in the streets with your ass. Is that bitch's pussy that good that you forgot how I held shit down for you? Nigga, I've been the one holding guns, transporting drugs from state to state, and doing bids for you. Nigga, don't stand here on your high horse like you better than me. We're both in the streets."

"That's the thing, Kimora. Maybe I don't want you in the streets. Did you ever think about having kids and being a stay at home wife? You're damn near twenty-five and still living life like a teenager. I'm a nigga. I can run the streets. I admit that shit turned me on in the beginning, but we're getting old. I no longer want you out in the streets with me. I want you home when I get here. No more clubbing all week, excessive drinking, popping pills or smoking weed like you're crazy. I'm ready to be a father and a husband."

"Well, you might as well go on ahead and be with that bitch. I'm not ready to be a mother, and your ass not ready to be a husband. Quiet as its kept, you've never been my husband. Hussein, you were more like my partner in crime. Miss me with that shit you saying right now because it's fake as fuck."

Without hesitation, I jumped up and wrapped my hand around her throat, not hard enough to hurt her, but enough to apply pressure. The more I squeezed, the more I realized it wasn't even worth it. She was stuck in one place, and I was in another. A nigga wanted more out of life. Don't get me wrong life is damn good, but I want it to be great. Sometimes the person you love and sleep next to every night can be your downfall. Just looking into Kimora's eyes, I knew she would be the death of me. Instead of arguing with her or laying my hands on her, I walked out the house on her dumb ass.

"Where are you going, motherfucker? Are you going to be with that bitch? I swear to God I'll make your life a living hell if I find out you with that homewrecking hoe. I knew you were still fucking that bitch. That's why I'm fucking somebody else. Go on ahead and play captain save a hoe. I guarantee you I won't be here waiting on your dog ass. I got a nigga that likes me face down and ass up so fuck you, Hussein!"

That last part pissed me off, not because she claimed to be fucking another nigga but because she was being disrespectful. Without a second thought, I pulled my gun out and let off a couple of rounds. The bitch forgot that I was the crazy one in this shit. She was just playing crazy.

"Keep talking, bitch! I'm gone make sure I hit your ass the next round. You're mouth gone get you murked, Kimora. Since that nigga like you face down ass up make sure he like you enough to let your tired pussy ass live with him. Get the fuck out my shit with your hoe ass!"

"I'm not going no motherfucking where! I guarantee you are though!" That bitch was still running off at the mouth.

Instead of me killing her ass, I hopped in my whip and left. When a bitch spits venom, it's time to get the fuck away from her. Kimora might as well pack her shit because I'm done with her ass. I'll never sleep under the same roof or fuck with her again. That bitch threatened my life, and she can't be trusted.

13

YOKA

I was more than ready to get this baby out of me. At six months, I was in more pain than I cared to deal with. Besides being in pain, I was so happy I was having a girl. I literally have not stopped shopping since I found out. A baby shower is out of the question because I have no one to come, so I've been making sure I have everything that I need.

At first, I wasn't thrilled about Sheik giving me a damn house, but now that I've actually made it a home, I love it. Surprisingly, Sheik barely comes over, but he makes sure he sends his right-hand man Max to make sure I was okay. I was so thankful just knowing that Sheik has given me a safe place to be. I've literally stopped living in fear of Zuri. If he's still looking for me, he needs to come on with it because I guarantee his ass is not ready.

In my spare time, I've been going to the gun range so that I can become more efficient. Never in my life did I think I would need a gun to defend myself against anyone, but after everything I've been through, it's necessary, not to mention my mother and myself being the victim of gun violence. I planned to protect my daughter and myself at all costs. I refuse to allow Zuri or anyone else to snatch me away from her.

After a long day of shopping, I pulled into the driveway and noticed a female standing on the porch. After a couple of seconds of trying to see who she was, I grabbed my gun from the glove compartment and slipped it in my purse. Although she had a pretty face, I couldn't trust her ass either. These bitches will set you up in a minute for a nigga if the price is right.

"Can I help you?"

"Actually, you can. I was trying to see who's squatting on my property." I looked at this bitch like she had lost her mind because obviously, she had. It was a good thing I always kept the deed that Sheik had given me. For some reason, I felt like it would come a time when I needed it. I just didn't think a damn female would show up to the house claiming it to be hers.

"There must be some mistake because this is my house. There ain't no squatting going on over here, baby." I handed her the papers, and I could tell she was shocked at what she was looking at.

"That motherfucker!"

"Wait a minute! Who are you?"

"I'm Mrs. Shakur. You must be the mistress." I shook my head and pinched the bridge of my nose to keep from going off on this bitch.

"Sorry, sweetie. Mistress isn't even in my vocabulary. I'm not sure what's going on with you and your husband, but you need to take that up with him. As you can see this is my house."

"Don't get comfortable. As a matter of fact, start looking for other living arrangements. I can assure you that you won't be living here long." She had tears in her eyes as she walked off. A part of me wanted to curse her the fuck out, but Mrs. Shakur was seriously hurt. She walked off with tears in her eyes. I'm not sure what the fuck is going on with them, and I don't care. All I know is that Sheik needed to handle this shit because that bitch will not be just popping off over here. Next time I won't be so calm about this shit.

As I went inside the house, I was having second doubts about taking this house from him. I should have known some shit would come behind this. Then again, I had to think logically. Sheik wouldn't give this house knowing it would cause drama. At first, I had plans on cursing his ass out, but instead, I'm going to call him and calmly tell him to check that bitter bitch.

~

"YOU REALLY NEED to stop sleeping so hard. One of these days you gone wake up dead," an unknown woman said as I walked into my kitchen.

"Who the hell are you?"

"My son told me you were a feisty one." She laughed, but I stood there looking at her like she was crazy. The more I watched her, the more I saw Sheik and Hussein in her.

"I don't mean any disrespect, but he didn't tell me that you were coming."

"He's away on business. I came over here to make sure you were okay, and that evil bitch didn't come over here fucking with you. So, I'll be here until he makes it back. By the way, I'm Retha. Come on sit down and eat this chicken I fried."

"Nice to meet you. I'm Ni'Yoka."

It was nine in the morning, and this woman was up frying chicken and fucking up my kitchen, not to mention drunk as fuck. I swear I need to move the hell out of this house.

"My son told me about you and your situation. If I were you, I would have waited until that nigga went to sleep and gave him an Al Green special."

"What's an Al Green special?"

"That's when you pour hot grits on a bitch for thinking it's cool to put they fucking hands on you. Don't ever let a nigga fuck with you and think he can have a good night's rest. Fuck that. I'm stabbing bitches in they sleep if I can't do it while they woke. Now sit down so that we can feed that baby. Plus, I need me a nap before *General Hospital* comes on. I have to be wide awake when Sonny Corinthos comes on the screen."

I had to laugh at her because she was so serious, not to mention she had turned up a can of beer like a damn whino. I could tell this lady was about to get live, and I was here for it. It has been a minute since I had entertainment from the comfort of my home. Actually, it has been a minute since I laughed at all.

As I sat at the table eating the chicken, I felt a warm rush of liquid come out of my vagina. I immediately jumped up and ran to the bathroom. I pulled my panties down, and it was blood and mucus mixed together. Panic set in because I knew this wasn't normal. I quickly cleaned myself up and got ready to head to the hospital. There was no pain or anything, but I wanted to be on the safe side.

"Are you okay?"

"I'm not sure, but I think I need to go to the hospital. I have blood and mucus coming out of me. I'm only six months pregnant, and I know this isn't normal."

"Lord, have mercy. Let me fix myself up and get you over there. I'm going to call Sheik and let him know."

"Don't call him. I don't want him worrying. This is not his responsibility to drop his business plans for. I'll be okay. My friend Seven can come with me because I don't want to burden you either."

I appreciated these people helping me, but at the same time, I didn't feel good about them going out of their way for me. It's something about burdening other people that gets to me. I just hate to do it.

"Girl, go get dressed and put your pride to the side. My son already told me you have no family here. So right now, we're your family. If he saw fit to protect you then it's only right I do the same. Hurry up because if that baby is coming out, he or she going to be in a fucked up situation because I'm drunk as fuck."

There was no arguing with this woman, so I got dressed and headed to the hospital with her drunk ass driving. She had called Sheik even though I told her not to. Now he's on his way to the hospital from wherever he was at. Seven wasn't answering her phone, and I really needed her support. I just hope she arrived before this lady drives me crazy.

∾

As I sat in the hospital bed, I was trying my best not to cry. However, the tears wouldn't stop flowing. At the moment, I was being prepped for an emergency C-section. My daughter was ready to come into the world, but I wasn't ready for that. There was a possibility that she could die or have developmental disabilities with being born prematurely. I don't know why God is punishing me this way. Lord, I don't know how much I could handle. Seven still hasn't arrived, and I need her now more than ever.

"Stop crying, Ni'Yoka. Both of my boys were born early, and they are fine. I know you don't know me from a can of paint, but I'm going hold your hand through everything. Now stop crying. It's almost time to meet your daughter. Do you have a name picked out?"

"No. I hadn't thought about it." As I wiped my tears, the staff came in and got ready to wheel me up to the delivery room.

"I would say a quick prayer for you baby, but I'm drunk right now. I can't be playing with God like that."

Ms. Retha not only had me laughing but the staff too. This lady was overly funny. Although we really didn't know each other, I was so happy she decided to be in the delivery room and support me.

14

SHEIK

It seemed like as soon as I left Miami shit went left. The fact that Azada showed up at the house I gave to Yoka had me hot. As far as I knew, she didn't even know about the house. Besides that, shit had my nerves all bad when my OG told me she had to have an emergency C-section. All I can do is feel like Azada is the cause of the shit. I'm not crazy though. Her momma is behind this shit. It's like these greedy bitches want to force my hand, and I'm trying to be civil in this situation. To make matters worse, this bitch got her lawyer calling me with demands and shit. This is not the battle that she wants to fight. I've tried to be cool and give her everything she asked for when we decided to part ways, but she's going to regret pulling this shit with me.

Although I wanted to head right back to Miami, I couldn't. A nigga had other business in the A that required my attention.

"Did Ma call back and say anything?" Hussein asked as he handed me the blunt we were smoking. We had been sitting inside of Zuri's OG's crib for hours waiting for her to come home. This nigga had basically disappeared off the map. Whoever was helping his ass hide was doing a damn good job of it, and I intended on getting at his ass.

"Nah! The surgery is probably still going on." I grabbed a Newport and flamed it up, which is something I long ago stopped doing, but I kept a fresh box in my glove compartment for when I was stressing.

"You must really be feeling Yoka. She's got you around this motherfucker trying to kill for her. Nigga, you so stressed out that you're sitting here smoking a blunt and a fucking cigarette.

"I told you there is nothing between us. She saved my life with that nigga Trill, so I owe her."

"Your ass is feeling her, and you know it. You might have her fooled with that nice shit, but I know you. Having her at the house gives you more access to her. Y'all might not be on shit now, but she's giving birth as we speak. It's a whole new ball game when she's running around looking thicker than a snicker."

"Don't worry about me, nigga. Worry about you and that crazy ass Seven."

"That girl has cut me off again. She's going to make me fuck her up. At the same time, I'll just fall back and give her the space she wants. Prior to Kimora and her crew attacking her, we weren't fucking around like that. We were on some friends shit. Honestly, big bro, she has me rethinking that whole idea. My heart is definitely not with Kimora anymore. That bitch showed me a side of her that has made me hate her ass. Never in my life did I think I would feel that way about her. Just thinking about that bitch makes me mad as fuck."

"Kimora ain't shit compared to Azada's money hungry ass. Let's go! She just pulled up." I put the cigarette out and pulled my hoodie tight. We both got out of the car and slowly crept up to the house. The shit was easier than I thought because we basically walked in the door without knocking.

"What the hell are y'all doing in my house? She reached for her purse, but I quickly flashed my gun.

"You don't want to do that. Have a seat?"

"Who are you and what do you want? I don't have any money so save yourself the trouble."

"Don't insult us, old bitch!" Hussein yelled. She quickly sat down on the couch.

"Now look. We're not here to hurt you, but we will. You see I'm the calm one. He's the not so calm one as you can see. I'm going to ask you this one time and one time only. Where the fuck is Zuri?"

"I haven't seen or heard from my son in months. He left his son here and never came back."

"Which kneecap should I shoot her in?" Hussein asked.

"The right one!"

"Ahhhhhhhh!" She fell in pain holding her bleeding knee.

"Next time it will be your head. Don't fucking lie to me. Where the fuck is your bitch ass son?" I spoke through gritted teeth.

"He won't tell me where he is, but he's no longer in Atlanta. He's on the run for the murder of his baby momma. He calls every week but never tells me where he is at. Please don't hurt me. Zuri is on the run, and I doubt if he's coming back here. Too much has happened."

The way she cried, I knew she was telling the truth. Just to get my point across and let her know that we weren't fucking around, I shot her old in the other knee for being stupid. She could have told us that shit from the jump.

"Tell his bitch ass that nigga they call Sheik is looking for him!" We left just as quickly as we came.

I drove nonstop back to Florida with nothing but Yoka on my mind. I hoped and prayed she and her baby were okay. The nigga Zuri could run, but he couldn't hide.

15

AZADA

When Sheik and I decided to go our separate ways, I was comfortable with it. In my heart, I knew he no longer loved me. As a woman, you feel that shit. It's all in the way he acts towards you. My only wish was that he had told me it was because he had a family. Just talking to that bitch at his house hurt my soul. I knew I had to get the fuck out of there because I felt like kicking her in her stomach. The only thing I could hear was that nigga in my head saying how he wasn't nutting inside of me. All of these years and he treated me like I was a bitch on the street. I think I could accept this shit had he told me from the jump instead of having me working on us. Had I known he was on some other shit, I never would have been so damn cool with asking for basically nothing. That nigga ain't got nothing but some money with mad change to spare. He's definitely going to pay for fucking over me. He got a whole bitch staying in a house that was acquired during our marriage. He thought I didn't know, but I knew.

Trust me he was not fucking with a fool. I shopped and stayed lit, but a bitch paid attention to everything. He forgot I was a con artist before I changed my life. Sometimes it doesn't pay to change your life for a nigga. They don't appreciate shit, but it's cool. I'll die before I let him have a good life with that bitch or that baby. Shit, was all good until I went through a file on the banker's desk. This nigga got all types of properties and shit. That's why he had no problem with giving me what I asked for. He had more where that shit came from.

"You still sitting in here sulking?" I rolled my eyes because my mother was wearing out her fucking welcome, not to mention constantly harping on this shit with Sheik. The last thing I needed was her throwing it in my face and saying how she told me so.

"I'm not sulking, Ma. I'm good on Sheik. He's going to get everything he deserves behind fucking me over."

"Get that weak shit out of here. You're talking too fucking soft for me. I hope you don't talk like that when y'all meet up with the lawyers. They're going to eat your ass alive in that room. Listen to me and listen to me good. You take that shit you found and produce it to your lawyer. I can't believe you only asked for fifty thousand dollars. Your ass is married to a fucking millionaire. I taught you better than to cheat yourself. Make that nigga pay you in cash, fuck tears. Now get dressed, you got a date." I looked at her like she was crazy talking about I got a date.

"With who, Ma?"

"Remember Butch?"

"Yeah, I remember him." I rolled my eyes because he was one of my mother's many conquests. Besides her being a master manipulator, she's also loose as a damn goose.

"Well, I've been back dealing with him, and he got this fine ass nigga that he's working for. He's new in town, and I told him I got a bad bitch that he would love. Butch is having a celebration tonight, and we're going to go. Wear something cute and sexy. I'm about to get dressed. Ohhh Muffin! This is just like old times. We're going to have so much fun."

I swear my mother was a teenager trapped in a forty-year-old woman's body. She kissed me on the cheek and rushed out of the room.

The last thing I wanted to do was deal with her and Butch's drunk ass. At the same time going out and kicking it would be good for me.

It's been a minute since I been out and had a drink. At this point, anything would suffice to get my mind off Sheik and his bitch.

~

"DAMN SHAY-SHAY! You never told me your daughter was a beautiful goddess. Where have you been all my life?"

I assumed this was the nigga she wanted me to meet. He wasn't all that, so I was lost as to why my momma put on like he was the shit. He looked slick as hell though like he could talk a cat off of a fish truck. He seemed like the type of nigga that had some shit up his sleeve, and you had to watch him all the time.

"Married to the wrong motherfucker!"

"Ma! Not cool."

"Girl, please! Fuck Sheik!"

I rolled my eyes at her because all night she had been embarrassing as fuck. I had never seen her drunk or loud in my life. Then I remembered Butch got high off of powder, and she was most likely high as a Georgia Pine with him.

"Fuck that nigga, ma! Let me show you how real niggas move." He grabbed my hand, and we walked away from everyone at the party.

"I don't even know you. How you just gone grab my hand?"

"I'm a boss baby. Now let me introduce myself. I'm Trigga. It's nice to meet you Azada. Don't look like that your OG told me all about you. Let me go grab us something to drink so that we can get to know each other better."

He stroked the side of my face with his soft hand, and he had me a tad bit smitten, but not so easily convinced. The charm he was trying to put on was off. I've come across bosses, and he wasn't one of them. A boss doesn't have to tell you he's a boss. With one look you can tell. I was cool on him, and I wasn't buying the bullshit he was trying to sell.

As soon as he walked away, I got the hell out of dodge. I didn't even tell my momma that I was leaving. She had pissed me off telling a perfect stranger my fucking business. I love and miss my momma, but I didn't like the new Shay-Shay. The old her would sit back and observe. This new person can't shut the fuck up. I hoped and prayed she moved in with Butch because I didn't want her ass at my house. Then again I might be just overreacting. I actually love her being there. It's just that I can't take her trying to turn me into the old me because I'm not that girl anymore. I'm not the smartest person, but he probably was a mark that she was trying to put me on to without telling me. She's good for that shit. I don't have time for sneaky shit right now. A bitch got bigger shit to worry about like how in the fuck I'm going to get Sheik to give more than what I initially asked for. The way he's sending threats, I already know it's not going to be easy, but I'm willing to fight for what I deserve, especially since he didn't see fit to fight for me.

As I drove home, all I could do was cry knowing that he had snaked me. The nigga had been in a relationship the entire time. The more I thought about it the madder I became. I had all intentions of going home, but I found myself at the gas station. I sat and thought long and hard before filling up two gas cans. The next thing I knew I was at that house he gave that bitch burning it to the ground. I didn't give a fuck if she was in there or not. If I can't have no happily ever after, I'll make sure she doesn't either.

16

SEVEN

I had been trying my best not to let Yoka know that her house had burned to the ground. Sheik was walking around about to lose his mind because he thought Zuri had done the shit. The fire department said that it was arson because they found gas cans on the premises. It was a damn shame this shit was happening right now. After all the work that had been put into the house, it was a shame the shit had went up in flames literally. For the first time since all this craziness started, I didn't believe Zuri was behind the shit. It's no coincidence that Sheik's wife showed up one day, and it was burned down the next. Both Sheik and Hussein had some problems on their hand with their bitches.

I had been looking at Yoka, and something was off with her. She had given birth to a beautiful baby girl, but we still hadn't seen her yet. With her being premature, her lungs hadn't fully developed, so they had her on a ventilator. I knew that she was worried, but she hadn't even given the baby a name yet. As a matter of fact, she looked depressed as fuck. I've never given birth, but I don't think postpartum depression is supposed to kick in this soon after birth.

Yoka was sitting in bed ignoring Sheik, his mom, and me. Ms. Retha had gotten so mad at her that she left. Sheik didn't pay the shit any attention. I guess that's because he was just glad she was okay, not to mention they weren't a couple, so he didn't have to be there for her emotionally. At the same time, I could tell that he wanted to be but didn't push the issue. I wasn't him or his momma. This bitch was not going to keep ignoring me, and she had just given birth to my goddaughter.

"Why are you ignoring everybody? I understand you worried about the baby, but that's not the way to go about it. You need to apologize to Sheik and his mother. I'm your best friend now talk to me and tell me what's going on."

"Nothing is going on. I'm just worried about my baby that's all. They won't even let me see her. What if something is wrong and they're not saying anything?" I leaned over and wiped the tears from her face.

"She's fine, Yoka. Trust me. If she wasn't, they would have been came and told you so. Now come on let's think of some baby names."

"Not right now, Seven. I just need some time alone to think about the fact that I'm a mother now. The shit still hasn't quite sunk in. Thanks for coming to be with me. I appreciate that shit." We embraced and at the same time, a nurse came in the room.

"Hey, mom. Would you like to go to the NICU to see your daughter?" A smile crept across Yoka's face, and I was so happy to see that.

"Yes. Can her godmother come too?"

"Absolutely!"

We helped Yoka into the wheelchair and headed to the NICU to see the baby. I think I was more excited than she was. I remember us being younger and talking about having kids. It's heartwarming to see at least one of our dreams come true. At the rate I'm going, it looks like I'll never get that. As we rolled passed the other babies, I immediately got baby fever. My heart also hurt for them because they all looked so tiny and sick.

"Here we are. I call her Diva because she has been acting real fussy and doesn't want to be bothered. She's a beauty, mom."

I had to do a double take looking at that baby. Something was off, and I mean seriously off. All I could do was shake my head as I looked at Yoka. Her face was showing what I was thinking.

"Do you have a life insurance policy, bitch?"

"Yeah. Why would you ask me that?

"I just want to make sure you have the proper funds to get put away nice because I can see you getting killed tonight and buried by morning. Bitch, it's about to be some smoke in the city. Are you going to tell him?"

"What are you talking about, Seven?"

"Stop fucking playing with me, Ni'Yoka. A blind man can see that isn't Zuri's baby. That's Sheik's baby, and you know it." I can't believe that she is the spitting image of him. Most newborns come out looking old as fuck but not this baby. Even with her being premature, the resemblance was uncanny. This baby didn't have an inch of Zuri inside of her.

"I swear to God I didn't know. We only had sex one time. Oh, my god! What the fuck is going on in my life?" she screamed so loud that caused the nurses to stop what they were doing and look at her.

"I don't know why you're sitting over there crying. This is a good thing. You already know that he's going to step up to the plate. I would rather him be her father than that motherfucker Zuri. She's gorgeous as fuck. I already know we gone have to fight cause all the little bald head girls gone be jealous of her." I stroked her face, and she cracked a smile.

"I don't doubt for a minute that he won't do the right thing, but how am I going to tell him that she's his."

"Do you want me to talk to him?" It wasn't my place, but as her best friend, I would do it with no problem.

"Nah! This is something that I have to do. Ain't that right, baby girl?" Yoka leaned over and kissed her. I stepped out of the room and let them have a moment to bond.

It warmed my heart to see my friend finally happy. At the same time, I was wondering would I ever get the chance to be a mom. Picture that Seven Santana being somebody momma.

Before heading back inside, my phone rang from an unknown

number. I answered, and it was a damn collect call from Hussein. He needed me to bail him out. Irritated wasn't a word for what I was feeling. All I wanted to know was why he didn't call his wife. I quickly walked back inside to tell Yoka

"Girl, guess who just called me."

"Who?"

"That damn Hussein asking me to come and bond his ass out! I'm not in the mood for that shit today. As far as I'm concerned he could sit his ass in there until his wife comes to get his ass."

I wasn't playing. For the first time, I didn't give a fuck about not being there when he needed me. It's something about going through shit with a man that will make you start not to give a fuck. Like I literally don't give a fuck at this point. In my heart, he hasn't done anything to me. I guess it's just that I harbor resentment towards him for not being emotionally available when I needed him. Yes, I know that he was married, and I shouldn't have been expecting more than he was able to give. At the same time, I felt like I deserved more from him.

"Go get that boy. When you got locked up, he brought me the money to get you without hesitation. Plus, Ms. Retha told me that they're no longer living together and headed to divorce court. He called you for a reason. Now stop being stubborn and bond him out. We will be fine. I promise to call you if I have to. Thanks for being here when I needed you the most. I love you, best friend."

"Awww! I love you too." We embraced, and I got ready to head down to the jail to bond his dumb ass out.

I swear every time I turn around Hussein is in jail. I'm starting to think he loves that shit. I'm surprised he even got a bond because he's on parole. I can't wait to hear the reason why he's locked up this time.

~

"It took your ass long enough. I called you hours ago."

"First of all, don't get in my car talking shit to me because I didn't have to come and get your black ass. Secondly, you should have called your wife. Thirdly, why the fuck are you in jail anyway?"

He had me fucked up getting in my car with a fucking attitude. As I drove away from the jail, a bitch had the right mind to turn around and happily drop him back off.

"I'm not in the mood for your smart ass mouth. Make this the last time you ever refer to that bitch as my wife. She's the reason a nigga was locked up and looking at heavy jail time."

"Wait a minute. What happened?"

"I'm in the crib getting some much-needed sleep. The next minute I know I'm hearing shit crashing and breaking. The police came in my shit hard. They found some guns and a pound of weed. The only reason I got a bond is because the judge grew up with my momma and did a solid for her. Man, I'm so mad I could kill this bitch. I'm facing ten years behind this shit!" He started punching the dashboard, and all I could do is let him get his anger out. I felt bad for getting all smart with him and shit.

"Calm down. I'm sure there is another alternative instead of jail time."

"Not this time, ma. I'm on parole so getting a bond was like a fucking miracle. With my fucking luck, ain't no more miracles around this bitch. You ain't got no weed in this bitch? I need to smoke."

"I got some at the crib."

"Good. That's where I planned on going anyway. A nigga needs peace of mind. Can you be my peace of mind like you used to be? I know I fucked up and hurt you. At the same time, I need you right now. My mind is mentally fucked up behind a lot of shit that's going on in my life. I just need my old friend to make me feel better."

We were stopped at a red light and Hussein took the opportunity to reach over and kiss me passionately. With no hesitation, I grabbed his face and allowed him to suck on my tongue. I loved when he did that. I felt the same butterflies I felt the first time we ever kissed. It's amazing how you can go from being mad at a person to loving them like crazy. In my mind, I knew I was one confused ass bitch in regards to this Hussein situation. Cars started to honk their horns, and we didn't break our kiss until we were ready to. The people just started going around us.

"Don't think you about to have me hostage in the house all weekend fucking me either."

"I'm about to lay so much pipe in that pussy that you're not going to want to go out."

I rolled my eyes at his ass because he was always so cocky. He had my pussy wet talking like that though. It had been a minute since I had some dick, so I was ready for him to go in for the kill, but he didn't have to know that.

As I headed to the house, so many things were going through my mind. His and Kimora's relationship was the main thing. I've heard him say before it was over between them. I couldn't help but wonder if this was just another one of those times when they were on bad terms.

"Keep it real with me. Are you and Kimora really done or is this just one of those times that y'all are into it? Let me know because I'm in a good place. The last thing I need is you coming back around and fucking up my spirit. I only want positive vibes around me. If you not on no real shit with me, then allow me to drop you off somewhere. I've told you before I'm no longer comfortable with being a mistress."

"I'm done with Kimora. I've already filed for divorce. If I weren't on no real shit with you, I never would have even called you to come and bail me out. I could have easily called my brother or my mother. I no longer want the type of love Kimora is giving. I chose to walk away for numerous reasons that I don't desire to get into. I have no plans to come in and interrupt your soul. All I want to do is snatch it. " He placed his hand on my leg and rubbed it.

As I drove all I could picture was my legs in the air and his head buried between my legs. The nigga was a beast with his tongue. That shit alone had me thinking about which corner of my house I would be sitting in rocking after he's done with my ass.

17

SHEIK

As I stood outside of the house I gave Yoka, I was in disbelief. I had burned completely down to the grown. I know that bitch Azada is behind the shit. No one else has a reason to go out of their way to burn the fucking house to the ground. Here I was trying to protect her from that bitch ass nigga, and now I have to protect her from Azada crazy ass too.

After paying the cleanup crew to clear out the rubble, I headed over to my lawyer's office to sit down with the bitch and her lawyer. It was going to take everything in me not to confront the bitch about what the fuck she did. I want to beat her ass, but I'm not trying to be in jail for no damn domestic violence charges. I would never put my hands on a lady, but I'll knock the fuck out of a bitch. As I walked into my lawyer's office, I made sure to be late. I wanted to torture the bitch as much as possible.

"How nice of you to finally join us," she said.

"Don't talk to me. As a matter of fact, don't look at me. Anything you got to say you need to say it to your lawyer, and he'll relay the message to my lawyer."

"It's a beautiful day outside. Why you want to come in here all flamed up and angry?" She winked at me and thought she was so cute playing with me. The fact that she made a reference to flames with a smirk on her face had me livid. The bitch knew what she was doing.

"Enough of the hostile exchanges, let's get down to the business at hand. Mrs. Shakur, what are you asking for now? My client is ready to get this done and over with."

"Prior to learning that my husband had a mistress and a baby on the way, I had no issue with us parting ways amicably. Now that I know about his secret his life, I want more. He has homes and businesses that were acquired during our marriage. Some of them I knew about and others I didn't. He has even gone so far as to move his bitch into one of the houses.

"She's not my mistress, and she's not pregnant by me. It's none of your fucking business who I give a house to. What makes you think you deserve more than what I've already given you. During our marriage, you never worked a day, not to mention you never lifted a finger to support me with those businesses. I don't owe you shit but a bullet in your fucking head for burning down that house." I was immediately pissed off because I had let that bitch beat me for my cool.

"Nigga, please! I haven't burned down anything. Here is a list of what I'm asking for. Give it to me, and I'll sign the divorce papers." The bitch handed my lawyer a piece of paper, and he handed to me.

I laughed because she went from wanting one property, to wanting two and one of the vacation homes. I couldn't do shit but laugh even harder because this bitch went from wanting fifty thousand to five hundred thousand. I sat and thought long and hard before giving her my answer. One thing for sure and two for certain I wanted this marriage done and over with. It really bothered me that she had resulted to greediness because I wished her the best. If she ever needed me, I wouldn't have had a problem with looking out for her. It's crazy how you can be sleeping next to the enemy and not even known it.

"You got it. Now sign the divorce papers." She smirked as she signed the papers. Had I been in the mood to play games with her ass, I would write the bitch a bad check and put the properties up for sale she was requesting.

"Are you sure, Mr. Shakur? We can do some more negotiating." My lawyer was a courtroom bully, so he was all for that negotiating shit. I just wanted to give the bitch what she wanted so that she could go on about her business.

"Some people are not worth the fight."

I placed my Versace shades on my face and walked the fuck out of there. Azada was no longer my wife, and that shit gave me a hard-on out of this world. Fuck that bitch and everything she stands for. If she knows what's good for her, she will move on with her life because I am not above murking her ass.

Since I have that out of the way, I can focus on trying to break the news to Yoka about the house being burned down. She's already in a funk about her baby being born premature, so this is the last thing she needs right now.

~

As I walked inside of the hospital, I hoped Yoka was in a better mood than she was yesterday. She got my OG mad as fuck at her. Ms. Retha is the last person whose bad side you want to be on. At the same time, I can tell that my mother is smitten with her. The way she spoke about being in the delivery room with her made me see how much she really wants to be a grandmother. At the rate Hussein and I are going, that shit ain't happening anytime soon.

When I entered her hospital room, she was sitting up in bed just staring off into space. She cracked a smile when she noticed that I had balloons and roses.

"Aww! Thank you so much."

"I'm glad to see you feeling better than yesterday. I hope you know my momma is mad at you."

"I know. She just called up here and read me my rights. Remind me never to get on her bad side again. I do want to apologize to you for my behavior yesterday. There was just so much going on all at once. You've been nothing but nice to me. You definitely deserve better than that. I hope you can forgive me."

"It's all good, champ. Besides all of that, how are you feeling? How is the baby doing?"

"I'm good besides this damn pain from the C-Section. She's fine. They have her on a ventilator due to her lungs being underdeveloped. She has jaundice, so they have her under the UV lights. She's doing better than they initially expected, so she's definitely a fighter."

"She's a fighter like her mother. I can't wait to meet her. I bet she's beautiful just like you."

"We need to talk, Sheik." She was staring down and twiddling her fingers. Yoka was never the one for nervousness, so looking at her nervous like this had me concerned.

"What's good? Holla at me."

"I don't think Zuri is my daughter's father. I took one look at her for the first time, and I know he's not her father."

"Do you at least have a clue to who it could be?"

"Yeah, I do. She looks just like you, Sheik." I quickly stood up and looked at her like she was crazy.

"You tripping. Take me to see her right motherfucking now! As a matter of fact, hold that thought. Let me call my OG up here. I need her to take a look too. For your sake, I hope you're not playing no motherfucking games because I'm not that type of nigga. This shit is serious. It's mind-boggling to me that you didn't know this shit prior to giving birth."

"Stop fucking yelling! You think I want this shit. Do you actually think I wanted to torture myself for months about Zuri being the father of my daughter? I hated myself for even being pregnant. So many days I prayed that I miscarried because I didn't want that evil nigga blood running through my baby's veins. I've been living in fear thinking he's coming to kidnap me again. Trust me. I'm not playing no games here. If you don't want to be her father, I don't give a fuck. I don't have nobody anyway. As far as I'm concerned, you can leave, nigga! I've already planned to raise her alone so trust me I'm not expecting shit from you!"

"Watch your motherfucking mouth! All that ain't even you. Fuck you getting all defensive for. Fuck waiting on my momma, tell these people to take us to her now! I'm done talking with your ass!" Yoka had me fucked up thinking all that slick shit she was spitting would ever slide. She has forgotten that she just dropped a fucking bombshell on me.

"What's all the yelling about? You guys have to keep it down you all are disturbing the other patients.

"We need to go to the nursery to see the baby immediately!" I demanded.

The nurse jumped with me yelling, but I didn't give a fuck. This shit had me throwed, and I needed to see what the fuck was good. My mind was on one thousand, and nobody could bring that shit down to one hundred. I was pissed, and the only thing that would calm me down would be seeing the baby.

"Right away." She quickly walked out of the room and came back to get us seconds later. I hated showing my other side to Yoka, but a nigga was angry as fuck.

"Wipe your face man!" I didn't mean to yell, but I had seen her cry more than smile and that weak shit was starting to bother me. I grabbed some tissue to wipe her face, but she snatched it from me. Seconds later, the nurse came back to get her.

"You can take him. I don't want to go." She folded her hands being stubborn, but I didn't care. Instead of pacifying her, I walked out to go see the baby. Yoka had better hope she was keeping real with me because she won't like the other side of me that will fuck her up.

After placing on the protective clothing they gave me, I was let inside the NICU to see her.

"She's your twin, dad. I'm glad you came to see her. Mom is not very enthusiastic about seeing her. If she's going to survive, she needs her mother's touch. Try talking to her about that. This is a very important time in your daughter's life. I've been her nurse since she was born. This is my little Diva here. She has personality too. I'll leave you alone to bond with her. This is the first time she's opened her eyes, so she's happy you're here, dad."

The nurse walked out and, I sat in the rocking chair in front of the plastic ass bed they had her in. I quickly took pictures of her with her eyes open. I sent a picture to my mother and to my brother with the caption: *Apparently, I'm a father. Does she look like me or what?"*

I sent one to Yoka as well so that she could see that her eyes were open.

"Hey, lil mama. I guess it is all about you now. You got to get better so you can cheer your momma up. She's going through it." I stroked her face, and she started moving around. It was good to see her moving around.

Just looking at her I knew things were about to change for me drastically. I needed to do some things make life good for Yoka. Looking at her, I knew I didn't need a blood test. She looks just like me when I was a baby.

After sitting with her for about an hour, I headed back up to Yoka's room. When I walked inside, an unknown man was talking to her.

"What's going on?"

"He's here to give you a paternity test."

"Man, get the fuck out of here! Did I ask you for a blood test? Did I ever say she wasn't mine? Stop it with the fuckery okay! You good, my nigga." He packed up the test kit and paperwork then promptly left the room.

"Are you sure? I don't want you coming around later on in life talking about a blood test."

"Let's get some shit straight right now. Lose that attitude because you are putting energy into the wrong shit. You need to have your ass down there in the NICU bonding with our fucking daughter. Going forward, think before you say some shit slick to me. I hate females with smart ass mouths. You're the mother of my daughter, so you need to act accordingly. I need you to become a responsible mother right now and not later. Put all that pride to the side and that attitude in your back pocket. Now, where is the birth certificate so that I can sign it?"

"She doesn't even have a name, Sheik? Plus, we can't sign it without a witness."

"What's her name Yoka? I felt stupid as hell down there calling her lil momma cause I didn't know her name."

"I haven't named her. I'll let you do the honors." I sat for a couple of minutes thinking of a name for her. Then the perfect name for her came to mind.

"Sheikerra Husani Shakur. What you think about that?"

"Ghetto as fuck, but I love it." It felt good to see her at least crack a smile, but I was still mad at her ass for coming at me reckless. At this point, there was no need for me to tell her about her house burning down. Her and my daughter was coming home with me, and I didn't give a fuck if she didn't want to. At this point, she had no say so in the matter. I was the captain of the fucking ship.

"Good. I'll be back later. I need to handle some shit. Call me if you need me. My momma is on her way up here to bring you food and sit with you. We'll talk when I get back. There is definitely some shit that needs to be discussed about our future." I kissed her on the forehead and headed out. A nigga needed to find a new house and beef up security. My baby girl was precious cargo. I needed to go and buy every AR-15 that I could find because I intended to protect my family at all cost. If a nigga was coming for me or my girls, they had better come correct. I was willing to do jail time or die behind what the fuck belonged to me. The bar has just been raised tremendously.

18

YOKA

It had been a week since I gave birth and I was finally able to go home. At first, I was so sad about my daughter having to stay behind, but I knew it was for the best. I had been sitting down in the hospital sanctuary just praying and asking God to cover my life. At this point, I didn't have room for any more of his surprises. He needed to show me a sign that I was going to be happy in my new life as a mom.

Sheik has been so attentive. He's almost too attentive for me. Now that he knows she's his daughter, he's become so damn bossy. It's starting to make me mad because he wants to make all of the decisions for her care without even consulting to me. I know he wants to be a responsible father, but we need to make decisions together as parents.

Honestly, it's cute seeing him be an overprotective father. Maybe it's just me, but our daughter has him acting differently. I can't really explain it. It's strange though. Besides that, I've been worried because I really don't know him like that. We've only had sex once, and we now share a daughter. It feels so weird and awkward. However, I'm grateful that he is her father and not Zuri. I know people are like bitch how could you not know. I swear to God I didn't know. Actually,

Sheik never even crossed my mind. My mind was so fucked up that I guess I wasn't thinking clearly about the timing.

After sitting and praying a little while longer, I headed back upstairs to the NICU. I wanted to spend as much time with my princess before I got ready to leave. She was only three pounds at birth, and she's gained one pound since. I'll be happy when I'm actually able to breastfeed her. She has so many tubes that I can't really do much. I still haven't held her, and that's torture. She's getting better and better every day. So, I know that it's will only be a matter of time before she'll be strong enough to go home.

"Stop crying, Yoka. Lil Momma will be just fine. With everybody alternating with sitting with her, she's cool. Plus, Max is standing guard while I get you home and settled in." I had been crying like crazy since we left the hospital. That shit was pure torture leaving her behind.

"I know. I'm just overreacting and overthinking as usual. I am happy to be going home so that I can sleep in my own bed without being woke up. I swear you can't get no damn sleep in the hospital."

"About your own bed. I have something to tell you. Don't be mad I just didn't want to worry you while you were in the hospital. You were under enough stress, and the last thing I wanted to do was add to it."

"What's going on, Sheik?" I didn't like the tone of his voice at all. I had a feeling God was about to make me question him again.

"Azada burned your house down, but don't worry. I have you a brand new house that's fully furnished. Seven and my OG got the house together, not to mention the nursery is off the chain."

"I don't want a new house, Sheik. I want my house with all of my important documents and shit. The only photos I had of my mother were in that house. I swear to God I'm going to kill that bitch!"

"Calm down. I handled her." He tried to touch my hand, but I knocked it away. He was too fucking calm for me.

I had lost shit that couldn't be replaced. I don't give a fuck what he's talking about. As soon as I am healed, I'm finding that bitch and fuck her up. She has disrespected me two times too many. The bitch will most definitely not get a third. I have every intention of having him think I'm cool with him handling it. He ain't handled shit because if he did, I would have my fucking house.

An hour later, we pulled up to a beautiful home that looked like it had its own island. I would usually be asking questions but not this time around. This bitch was lavish. If this was the house that he had purchased for our daughter and me, the nigga wouldn't hear another word. This place was three times bigger than the house he had given me. Azada dumb ass had actually helped me. I might spare her the ass whooping she's got coming after all.

"Welcome to our new home." Wait a minute did he say *our*?

"Our home?" I questioned.

"What? You thought I would have you and my daughter living alone. Hell nah? I need to make sure my girls are well protected at all times. Plus, she deserves to grow up in a house with both of her parents. I didn't have that, and I don't want that for her. It's like her being here has given me a new purpose in life. I just want to live better and do better in life. Here I got this for you." He handed me a Tiffany & Co bag, and I looked at him funny as I grabbed the velvet box. I opened it, and it was the most beautiful ring I had ever seen.

"What's this for, Sheik?"

"It's a promise ring. I promise to always be here for y'all. No matter what I'm going to do my best by you and our daughter." My heart fluttered as he placed it on my finger. The diamonds were shining so bright, and I was so speechless. Sheik was always so full of surprises. Just when I think his heart couldn't get any bigger, it does.

"This is too much, Sheik. How could I ever repay you? I mean you've literally been going out your way for me, and we're not even a couple. Not that I wouldn't want to be with you, it's just that we met under crazy circumstances. Now we share a daughter, and you're ready to jump into being a responsible father. You've done so much that I just don't think there is anything I can give you for all that you've done for me."

There I was again crying, but these were happy tears. I had been questioning God and what he was doing in my life. All along my pot of gold at the end of the rainbow had been in front of me all along. I was starting to think the key to my happiness lied with Sheikem Shakur.

"You don't owe me anything. As a matter of fact, you've already paid me for a lifetime. Shiekerra is all a nigga needs but having the both of you would make my life even better. Let's give this life a try together. I know we can do it. Of course, there will be bumps in the road. Relationships aren't perfect, but as long as we're together, we can perfect it. A nigga don't want you just to be a baby momma. I'm coming to pick her up, you calling for shit she needs. Hell nah! I want us in the house together. It's too many niggas out here comfortable with their seeds only coming over on the weekend. I want my daughter in the crib with me twenty-four seven, three hundred and sixty-five days a year. I know a nigga wasn't truthful when we hooked up, and I apologize for that. I just hope you give a nigga a chance to show you that I can be the nigga you want and the father she needs." Sheik had said a mouthful, and he had my undivided attention. For the first time in a long time, I felt loved.

"To be honest. You had me the moment we met at that gas station. I just didn't know it." I leaned over and kissed him passionately.

"Come on. Let's go inside. I'm excited for you to see the house."

He got out of the car and came around to open my door. Before I got out good, he had lifted me off of the ground and kissed me with so much force.

"Come on. I'm excited to see it." I jumped down and damned near pulled his arm off trying to get inside. Before I could touch the handle, the door opened.

"Surprise!" Seven yelled.

I covered my mouth in shock because they had thrown me a baby shower. Gifts were everywhere, not to mention there were people there I didn't even know. I guess they were Sheik's people. Either way, I was glad everyone came and did something nice for me.

"I just don't think I can cry anymore. This is too much." Seven reached her arms out, and we hugged one another tightly.

"Stop them tears Sis. This is a happy occasion. Welcome to the family."

"Thanks, Hussein. I appreciate it."

"Come on upstairs so that you can change your clothes." Ms. Retha grabbed my hand and led me upstairs.

This was all a dream that I never wanted to wake up from. This time last year I was probably somewhere getting my ass whooped or crying myself to sleep. If someone had told me that there was hope for me after everything I've been through, I would have told them that they were lying. I asked God for a sign, and he's showing me right now. I can't wait for my daughter to come home and experience the life her father is giving us.

19

KIMORA

The last thing I wanted was to get Hussein locked up, but he left me no choice. He was trying to carry me like a was a random bitch, and I wasn't having it. The nigga had to be reminded who the fuck I was. After everything we had been together, he had switched up on me, and I didn't like that shit. Never in the course of our relationship has he ever let a bitch come between our bond. However, this hoe Seven got him acting all brand new on me. That nigga better straighten up and act like he knows what the fuck it is. He caught a small break by getting a bond this time. If he doesn't get his together, it won't be a bond or an out date. I plan on sending the bitch to jail for the rest of his life. If he's not trying to be happy with me, I'll go to the end of the earth to make sure he won't be happy period. Hussein must have forgotten who I am, but I have every intention of reminding him.

~

"WHY THE FUCK you banging on my door like that?" Ms. Retha yelled as she opened the door. It was obvious she was drunk, and it wasn't even twelve in the afternoon.

"Tell Hussein to come outside, or I'm coming in there to get him."

"You and what army? Kimora, get back in your car and go home. It's too early in the morning for me to be handing out an ass whooping. That's exactly what you gone get if you cross my threshold. I know you in your feelings about the divorce, but don't let that shit cloud your judgment."

"We're not getting a divorce. I came over here to get him so that we can go home and fix this."

"You should have thought about that before you had him arrested. You're a fucking rat, and you know how he feels about that shit. I'm lost as to why you would do some shit like that. Baby, you ain't no real bitch. You're walking around here acting like you this big bad ass gangsta bitch, but you're weak. Kimora, you let your hurt dictate your mind. All of the credibility you earned in the streets don't mean shit anymore. You and I both know a rat s the worst thing a person can be labeled ass. I should be handing your ass some cheese. Save yourself the heartache and move on because my son has. Get the fuck off my property! Rats will be shot!"

That old bitch slammed the door in my face, and it took everything inside of me not to shoot it off the hinges. This nigga Hussein was really trying my hand. If he knows like I know, he'd come his ass around and fix our relationship. He's all that I know, and I refuse to live without him. It didn't take a rocket scientist to know he was most likely laid up with that bitch. I guess beating her ass wasn't enough. Her and Hussein have left me no choice but to up the ante.

For weeks I had been following him and the bitch Seven. So many times I wanted to hop out the car and kill both of them, but I couldn't. At the same time, I was hurt looking at him. I guess the shit he was asking of me he was getting from her. So many times I wanted to just drive away and go on with my life, but I couldn't. I felt like he was betraying me. In my mind all of those years of standing in the paint with him were nothing. How could he just throw away everything without even giving me a chance? It was him who wanted a self-proclaimed bad bitch, and that's what I became. He wanted a ride or die bitch, and that's what he got. Now he's switching up the game plan, and I can't just let the shit go like that. I've fought charges with him, I've done time for him, and I've pulled the trigger for him. Call me bitter all you want, but I can't let that nigga get down on me like that. Having me actually served with divorce papers makes my decision easier. Never in a million years did I think I would be having this types of thoughts. I'm living proof that a scorned woman is also a dangerous woman.

Shan Presents March Mayhem Contest!

SECRET CODE: SP0300103

Want a chance to win a $10 gift card, be sure to one click this hot new release, find the secret code, and email it to spreadingcontests@gmail.com. NO SCREENSHOTS! Be sure to hold on to your code, and watch out for all of Shan Presents releases between 03/1-03-31 to collect all the codes for your chance to be entered to win one of 5 cash prizes!

20

HUSSEIN

Going back and forth to court was weighing heavy on a nigga. If I took the shit to trial and got found guilty, I could be facing ten to fifteen years off top. If I plead guilty, I'll be coming home in under four years. I had a big decision to make. The shit was hella fucked up because Seven and I had become solid as fuck. Being with her made life easier. Even with knowing that I was facing another prison sentence she was willing to ride it out with me again. I just feel fucked up because she too good to be visiting a nigga in jail. She's been a nigga's rock, and I just want to show her how much I appreciate her. A nigga wanted to propose, but I was still legally married to Kimora, and that bitch was dodging me. I should have known she wasn't going to go peacefully. I had been looking for her so I could at least have a proper sit down with her and give her whatever assets she asked for. Although she was no longer what I wanted, she had helped me get money over the years. Although she was a rat ass bitch, the nigga in me that had that bond with her felt like she deserved something. On the other hand, I didn't want to even cross paths with the bitch after the shit she pulled. Each and every time I think about her calling the laws on me that shit makes me angry. That added with the fact that I couldn't find her made me wonder if the bitch was somewhere telling some shit as we speak. Thinking about the shit made me feel the need to talk to my big bro and get advice.

"How is my niece doing?"

"She's good. Getting fat as hell. They say she should be coming home in a couple of weeks. I can't wait because Yoka needs that baby home in order to cheer up. We've been good, but I can tell being away from Lil Momma has her all in her feelings. What's good with you and Seven?"

"We good. Hell, we would be even better if I could find that bitch Kimora. That added with these years that I'm facing has a nigga going through it. That's actually what I came over here to talk to you about. Do you think that bitch told the police about the other shit we have going on?"

"We won't know that until the police come kicking our shit in. I told you a long time ago to stop that bitch from being in our business. I fucked with her, but I kept my business separate from that. Azada doesn't know shit about what I do in the streets. I only let her ass know what I wanted her to know. The less your bitch knows about you, the less she can tell the laws. That's the same way I'm going to be with Yoka. I don't want her even knowing I traffic drugs and run guns. I need her to focus on being a mother and being the wife I need. You need to start building a family with Seven and focusing on the future. Don't make the same mistake twice. Keep Seven out of your business. All she needs to know is where your stash at in case you get into a bind nothing else. You have to have your personal life separate from business. Kimora ain't crazy, bro. She's probably somewhere licking her wounds, knowing she has fucked up. Fuck Kimora and focus on your relationship. You can stop worrying about jail time too. I've been making some calls to some of our friends at the states attorney's office. Shit will work out in your favor. I need you out here in the world helping me get this bread."

I should have known my big bro would know exactly what to say to calm my nerves. One thing for sure and two for certain I would never put Seven in my street shit. Honestly, there have been times when we weren't together she would do a run with me, but going forward that shit wouldn't be happening.

"Thanks, bro."

We sat and shot the breeze a little while longer, and then I headed home. Seven was most likely already home, and I promised her we would be going out to dinner to celebrate her promotion to supervisor.

Once I got into the car, I realized I had left my phone by mistake. There were several missed calls from Seven. When I tried calling back, there was no answer. I shook my head because I knew she was getting me back from not answering when she calls. Seven is the queen of petty. I'm thinking about spending the rest of my life with her, and she's going to have to change that shit and fast.

When I pulled up to the house, I was glad to see that Seven was home. Without hesitation, I quickly got out of the car and headed into the house. I was taken aback looking at Kimora holding Seven at gunpoint.

"Honey you're home," Kimora said devilishly.

"Kimora what the fuck you doing in here?"

"I'm the only one asking questions. Ain't that right, Seven?"

"Hussein, get this crazy bitch out of here!"

"Just calm down, Kimora. Put that gun down and stop pointing at her. I'm the one you're mad at so point it at me."

"Nah! I won't stop pointing it at her. This is all of her fault. I asked the bitch nicely to leave my husband alone, but she couldn't do that. This shit ain't right Hussein. After everything I've done for you, I can't believe you would just up and walk out on me. All the chances I've given you, and you couldn't even return the favor."

Looking at mascara running down her face let me know that this bitch was indeed mentally unstable. I was trying to think of a way to get the gun out of her hand without it going off.

"Kimora, you called the police and had me arrested. Did you

really think that things would ever go back to normal after that? Come on now. I told you what I wanted, and you denied me that, so I walked the fuck out. You're in here acting like I just up and left you. You and I both know that's not what the fuck happened. Put that gun down and stop this shit. We can sit here and come to some type of divorce agreement. I'll give you whatever you want, but you have got to put that fucking gun down."

"So, you're divorcing me?"

"I'm sorry Kimora. You've left me no choice."

"And you left me no choice!"

I didn't even have to react before she pulled the trigger and hit Seven in the chest. Without hesitation, she put the gun to her head and blew her brains out. I stood shocked and stunned at what the fuck had just unfolded in front of me. I couldn't believe Kimora had just went out like this. She was supposed to be stronger than this.

"Hussein, help me." Seven was struggling to talk and breathe.

"Shhhh! Don't talk. I'm getting you some help right now. Hold on, baby! Don't you leave me!" I held her applied pressure to the gunshot wound until the EMS could arrive. She wasn't looking good at all, but I was holding out faith that she was going to make it.

Instead of the police allowing me to go to the hospital, I was taken in for questioning. Kimora had really fucked me up with this one. Every time I close my eyes, I see her damn brains flying out of her head. As I sat inside of the interrogation room, I kept beating myself because I never should have triggered her. That shit was so dumb on my part. She was in a vulnerable state, and I should have been thinking clearly. This shit is all of my fault. Kimora is in the fucking morgue and Seven is fighting for her fucking life. I made a bad ass judgment call, and everybody is suffering behind it.

21

YOKA

Finding out that Seven had been shot had me hauling ass to the hospital. I was literally the only family she had as well. She grew up in and out of foster all of her life. On the way over to the hospital, all I could think about was what I would do if she didn't make it. Just when shit was going right, a monkey wrench comes out of nowhere and knocks shit all off balance.

As soon as I walked inside of the emergency department, Ms. Retha came rushing towards me.

"What are they saying?"

"Nothing yet. I can't believe this shit is happening. Where is Sheik?" For the first time since I had met this woman she was sober and showing emotion.

"He took a lawyer down to the jail for Hussein. He will be here as soon as he can. This shit cannot be happening. Why did she have to shoot her? Jumping on her wasn't enough. She just had to come back and shoot her."

I was trying my best not to cry because at this moment Seven needed for me to be strong for her but the shit was hard. The shit had me thinking if fucking with these married ass niggas was worth our lives. If the bitch Kimora could actually shoot Seven and kill herself, there is no telling what Azada has up her sleeve. I mean the bitch did burn my damn house down. Being with these niggas is not worth our fucking life.

"Come on over here and sit down." Ms. Retha grabbed me by the hand, and we sat waiting for someone to tell us something about her condition.

"I don't know what I would do if she doesn't make it."

"Stop talking like that and have some faith. If you don't have faith, you don't have shit. Seven is a strong girl, and she will survive this."

I covered my face with my hands and asked God to cover my friend. I needed her more than anything. My daughter was getting released from the hospital, and she needed her god momma to be here. Life is so crazy and ironic. Months ago I had been shot, and here we are now, and she's been shot. What are the odds of some shit like this happening?

"Excuse, ma'am. Are you Seven Santana's next of kin?" a male doctor came out and asked Ms. Retha.

"Yes. I'm her mother-in-law. Please tell me that she's going to be okay." She grabbed my hand and squeezed hard as she could.

"Ms. Santana is very lucky. The bullet was two inches from her heart. She was brought in just in time. Unfortunately, we weren't able to save her fetus. She has been taken up to the intensive care unit. Right now she's heavily sedated so she will be out of it for a while."

I breathed a sigh of relief hearing that she was going to be okay. At the same time, I felt bad that she had lost her baby. She hadn't told anything about being pregnant, so it was a good chance she didn't know.

"I'm going to call Sheik and let him know what's going on. I'll try my best to wait until you come down before I leave, but this is too much for me, and I need a damn drink. I'm glad she's okay, but now I have to worry about my son. He's a grown man, but I know he's fucked up behind what happened today. Stop worrying and go sit with my grandbaby. Give her a kiss for me."

"Okay, Ms. Retha. I'll be back as soon as I can. They've been calling me like crazy. If Sheik calls, let him know where I am because my phone doesn't work up there. The last thing I need is to hear his mouth about me not answering my phone."

As I rode the elevator up to the nursery, I wondered how much more Seven and I could take. At this point, I don't know how much more I can take. Besides that, I'm grateful for my friend still being here. This shit could have definitely been tragic. It's a good thing Kimora killed herself because I was definitely going to murder the bitch when I got my hands on her. I still can't believe she did that shit. Then again love is a very powerful thing. Everything you tell yourself you would never do you end up doing.

I ENDED up sitting with my daughter longer than I expected. She was fussy and very cranky. I simply hated to leave when she cried. The nurse kept telling me it was okay to leave, but I felt like I was being a bad mother by leaving her like that. She's going to be spoiled because I simply hate to hear her cry. Once she went to sleep, I headed to see Seven.

When I walked inside her room, I became so angry. Her father was in the room leaning over her bed. It would have been cool if he was an actual concerned parent but he's not. He's a fucking pedophile who used to rape and her as a kid. Last we heard he was in prison so him being here is a surprise. The sound of the toilet flushing made me look and see that her old ass grandma was coming out the bathroom. I never liked her old ass because she knew her son was raping Seven. When Seven's mother passed away from cancer, her father's mother got custody of her. One of the times he molested her she caught him in the process and beat the fuck out of him with a broom. Instead of calling the police and reporting the shit, she allowed him to continue to live in the home with him. For that, I have no respect for her old ass.

"I'm sorry, but she can't have any visitors right now," her grandmother said.

"Good thing I'm family and not a visitor." I rushed over to her bedside and kissed her on the forehead. She was still out of it and looked pale as ever.

"She can only have two visitors at a time," her father said.

"Why? You want me to leave so your creep ass can molest her and so your old ass can watch!" I was loud as fuck, and I didn't give a fuck. These people were sick, and I refused to leave my friend here with them.

"Quit all of that blasphemy girl!" her grandmother yelled as she grabbed a bible from her purse. God should have struck her ass down for playing with the word.

"You don't know what the hell you're talking about. Who the fuck do you think you are coming in here spreading lies like that?" Her father walked towards me but a nurse came into the room, and he stopped in his tracks.

"This is too much noise for the patient. What's going on in here? I don't remember you checking in at the nurse's station with me. Do you have a visiting pass?" the nurse asked me.

I quickly rolled my eyes and got pissed because I knew she was going to make me leave. I didn't have a damn visiting pass.

"No. I don't have a visiting pass."

"I'm sorry, but you will have to wait in the family area until one of them leaves. It's two visitors at a time. You all have to keep that noise down. We have a lot of sick patients and their families on this floor. "

As much as I wanted to argue with these people, I decided not to and just go down to the waiting area. Her father was so creepy to me. His presence alone made me uneasy. Seven needed to wake up so that she could tell the hospital to put their asses out. To my knowledge, she doesn't even deal with them, so I'm confused as to how they even know that she had been shot.

Once I made it down to the lobby, they announced that visiting hours were over soon, and I knew they weren't going to come down so that I could visit.

Since Ms. Retha was already gone, I decided just to go home. I was tired as hell and in need of some rest. The events of the day had taken a toll on my body. Come to think of it I haven't really had a good night's rest since I gave birth. A glass of wine and hot bubble bath would do my body good. On the drive home, I hoped and prayed Sheik was home. I was missing him like crazy. Since becoming official, I get to see just how busy of a man he is. I know that he own a lot of real estate, so it requires him to check on the properties. That added with the drug empire he runs, it's a wonder he makes it home in time for dinner. As busy as he is, he makes sure to go and sit with our daughter for a couple of hours a day, twice a day. One of the things I love most about him these days is the fact that family comes first. No matter how busy he is, he makes it a priority to check on us throughout the day. Besides missing Sheik on a daily I absolutely love being his better half. I never knew love like this before.

With him, I feel safe, secure, beautiful, important, and worthy. He goes out of his way to make me know that he's the lucky one to have me and not the other way around. Although we're still early in our relationship, I can see me with him for the rest of my life. Without doubt or question. That man makes me feel like a little girl in love each and every time he comes into the room. My heart races when I hear his car pull into the driveway. When he kisses me, I get butterflies in my stomach. Had I known he had the power to make me smile again, I would have been hopped at the chance to be his woman. I hate to admit it, but I'm glad his divorce is final. Now I can truly see a future with us. For years I shacked up with a man who gave false promises of marriage. With Sheik he lets me know that the possibilities are endless with us. The only thing that matters is my daughter and me. Just knowing how protective he is over us makes me want to follow wherever he leads me to. It's safe to say that I'm in love, and I don't care who knows about it.

Since it wasn't too late to cook when I made it to the house, I hooked up something quick— baked barbecue chicken, smothered potatoes, and string beans. Cooking was another thing that I loved to do. At a young age, my mother had me cooking, washing, and cleaning the house. As I sipped my wine standing at the island, I became sad as ever. Thoughts of my mother consumed me. One minute I was cool, and the next I was crying my eyes out.

"Baby! What's wrong?" Sheik rushed inside the kitchen and pulled me up from the floor.

"Why did he have to kill her like that?" As I wrapped my arms around his neck, I realized I hadn't cried over my mother's death like I should have. In this moment all my emotions had just spilled out of me.

"Stop all that ugly ass crying. I can't take that shit, Yoka. I didn't know your mother personally, but I highly doubt she would want you crying like this."

He was so strong that he lifted me up and sat me on top of the counter. I felt like a little girl whose father was consoling her. He grabbed some paper towels and wiped my tears. I instantly felt better. At the same time, a feeling of dread came over me. The feeling was unexplainable.

"Promise me you won't ever leave us."

"I promise, Yoka. You and my daughter are everything to me. I'm not going anywhere. Come on let's go upstairs." He helped me down, and that's when I remembered that I had cooked him dinner.

"Eat some dinner first."

"I am about to eat dinner. Trust me your pussy taste better." I couldn't do nothing but blush as he led me up the stairs.

I closed my eyes as he gently laid me down on the bed. I bit my bottom lip as he tugged at my pants to get them down.

"Look at me, Yoka!" he demanded.

I opened my eyes and looked down as he ripped my panties off of me. My heart raced, and my breathing became labored as he kissed my inner thighs. I didn't have breathing issues, but the feeling of him flicking his tongue back and forth against my clit had my ass hyperventilating. It was all too much happening at once, and I couldn't take it. Our eyes had been locked on one another as he devoured my pussy. To keep from screaming out in pleasure, I had to grab a pillow and place it over my face. I gripped the sheets as he inserted two fingers inside of me. I couldn't function as he methodically finger fucked me while sucking on my clit. It didn't take long for me to cum all over the place. I tried to calm my body down, but the euphoria from coming had me shaking uncontrollably. The shit was embarrassing but felt good as fuck.

"Don't fight that shit! Open your legs. I want to see that pussy talking to me." Sheik had a way with words no matter the situation. However, he didn't have to ask me twice.

I opened my legs and became a tad bit braver. I parted my pussy lips so he could see my juices flowing. As he undressed, I watched as his dick grew. He seductively stroked it until it reached its peak. I had no other choice but to spread my legs wider. All of that shy shit had to go out of the window. Sheik was a different caliber of man. He probably had mad bitches throwing the pussy at him. I had to step my bedroom game all the way up in order to keep him satisfied. I tried to get up, but he pushed me back down and roughly pulled me to the edge of the bed.

"We need to get a condom. I'm not on any birth control." He slowly slid inside of me and began to thrust as he spoke to me.

"You my woman, right?"

"Yes!"

"This my pussy, right?"

"Yes!"

"I got this. Just lay back, point your legs to the sky, and let me get up in there." Doing as I was told Sheik began to fuck me mercilessly. I was still sore from my C-section so that shit was painful, but it felt too damn good to stop him. I felt myself cumming all over his dick.

"Grrrrr!" he grunted as he came long and hard.

As I laid there taking it all in, I couldn't help but worry about if this nigga had got me pregnant. If I were pregnant, it would serve my dumb ass right. I could no longer talk about Seven. I was officially dick silly. Once Sheik was satisfied, he climbed next to me in bed, and I snuggled underneath him, not long after he started to snore softly. His phone started ringing, and I just knew he was about to get up and leave.

"Are you going to get that phone? It could be your mom or Hussein?"

"Nah! They cool I just left them. Fuck that phone! Whoever it is can wait until morning. I'd rather lay up under you." He kissed my neck a couple of times and went back to sleep.

As we both laid there, I couldn't fall asleep because his phone was going off. I started to think it could have been an emergency, so I jumped up to answer it. I usually never touch his phone, but the ringing was driving a bitch crazy. When I made it over to the dresser, it stopped ringing. I rolled my eyes when I saw that it was Azada. That piqued my interest because I wanted to know why the fuck she was calling him. They were divorced and as far as I knew they were no longer an item. Everything in me screamed to call that bitch back, but I followed my first mind. The last time I went looking for shit I hurt myself. I looked over at him sleeping naked and put the phone down. The bitch Azada didn't matter. Sheik was my man and the father of my daughter. I climbed back in bed with my man and laid on his chest.

22

AZADA

I had been calling Sheik like crazy because at this point he was the only person I could turn to. After our divorce proceedings I dealt with the fact that it was over between us. For some reason I started feeling bad behind letting my mother talk me into being greedy. That shit was wrong. At the same time I won't act like I wasn't hurt behind him having a baby with someone else. The sad part about it is that he lied about the shit. I've been seeing pictures of him, her and their beautiful daughter. As much larceny as I would like to have in my heart for him I simply can't. Truthfully, Sheik was a good man to me. I fucked up by taking him for granted and when I tried to do the right thing it was too late. I'm sorry for my behavior but now I understand where he was coming from. He wished me well when we separated and I should have done the same even if it wasn't with me. I'm kicking myself in the ass because I should have listened to Sheik when he told me to watch my momma.

She had been staying with me then all of a sudden she abruptly moved out on me without a word. I was happy as fuck so I decided not to press the issue and reach out to her. That was all fine and dandy until I checked one of my secret accounts and it had been depleted.

Two hundred thousand dollars was gone and I know she took my shit. I've always known that she was a fucking thief and she didn't give a fuck. As her daughter I would think that she wouldn't do that shit to me. Mainly because she has never took anything from me. We take shit from people together. I should have known shit would go south when she hooked back up with Butch. The last couple of weeks she's been high out of her fucking mind. Her ass has almost been zombie like. One day I could have sworn she came in the house with bruises all over her face. She kept saying that I was tripping but I know that I wasn't.

The sound of someone banging on my door made me rush to answer it. It was Sheik and I was happy as hell to see him. I quickly opened the door and he immediately started going in on me.

"Why the fuck are you calling me Azada?"

"I'm sorry to bother you but you were right about my mother. She stole two hundred thousand dollars from me." I didn't even mean to cry but I couldn't hold it in. I was kicking my own ass for the decisions I had made.

"I told your ass the bitch wasn't right so I'm lost as to why you called me. We're not married anymore and you aren't my responsibility. You allowed that bitch to come in and get in your head. So, whatever the fuck happened to you that's what the fuck you get. Don't call me any more with this bullshit. Take my advice and chop that shit up as a loss. While you're at it let your momma stay where the fuck she at. You crossed me Azada so it ain't shit I got for you. Being greedy is not cool at all and this just goes to show you. Be careful who you fuck over because you could meet that same fate. I have no ill feelings towards you but I don't even want you as a friend. Once a snake always a fucking snake.

I found a woman who's everything and more. Not to mention has given me the best gift a nigga could ask for in the form of a daughter. All of me is invested in Yoka and our daughter. I shouldn't even be here talking to you but I'm here anyway. A nigga had to come here and let your ass know to never bite the motherfucking hand that feeds you. I wish you the best in life but I've moved on with mine.

Don't call my phone anymore. As a matter of fact if you see me in the streets don't even speak."

"Sheik! Please just listen to me! I don't want anything from you. I just need you to hear what I have to say and why I was calling you!" I didn't mean to cry but the way he was talking to me really hurt. He pushed me off of him and walked out of the door. I just wanted to tell him that I was sorry and that he was right. This thing with my mother had me worried. I felt like something bad was about to happen but I couldn't put my finger on it. As much as I wanted to run behind Sheik I knew I couldn't. The bond we did have was gone he moved on and he hated me. I had no one to blame but myself. Our divorce was officially final so he owed me nothing. Not that I wanted anything. I just wanted him to hear me out.

The more I thought about my mother the angrier I became. I grabbed my car keys and got ready to head over to Butch house. I knew Shay-Shay was over there. She's bold with her shit so I know she's not hiding from me. As a matter of fact she's going to deny that she even took the shit. I swear I would beat the shit out of her with no problem from taking my shit with her scandalous ass. I could care less about her being my mother because the bitch didn't care about me being her daughter.

As I opened the door to leave out I was stopped in my tracks. It was the dud my mother tried to hook me up with at Butch house.

"What's up Ma?" He said as he basically shoved me back into the house.

"How in the hell do you know where I stay at?" I was trying my best to remember his name but I couldn't.

"You didn't get the memo about who the fuck who I am. Now I know Shay-Shay told you I was running shit around this motherfucker!"

"I don't give a fuck what you run my nigga. Now could you please leave so that I can go?" I tried moving pass him but without warning he punched me in my mouth.

"Motherfucker!" I tried fighting him but he was strong as fuck. He picked me up and basically body slammed on the floor. It felt like the wind had got knocked out of me. I managed to get up to my knees and crawl away from him but I didn't get very far.

"Didn't your trifling ass momma tell you its rude to walk out on a date?" I was trying to process what he was saying. This nigga was in here pressed because I walked out on his ass. When were we on a date because I missed that memo? The look in his eyes scared the fuck out of me and I knew he was capable of truly hurting me.

"Please leave I won't tell anyone about this. I'm sorry I left I just wasn't in the mood to for a date." He started laughing like a manic and pulled a gun from his back. I immediately tried to scoot away from him as he pointed the gun at me.

"That's what's wrong with bitches. They think they have a choice in what the fuck they want. Like I told you before I'm running shit." I saw the fire from the gun before the bullet even hit me. As I laid on my marble floor bleeding out I watched as he emptied my purse and took my debit, credit cards, and all of my money. My life was slipping away slowly but surely and all I could think about was why this nigga did this to me. I closed my eyes and tried to fight the inevitable. In the process I just asked God to forgive me for all of my sins.

23

SHAY-SHAY

As I sat in front of my vanity in my new home, I couldn't help but feel fucked up about taking money from my baby. At the same time I feel like she wouldn't miss it. Her ass was sitting on bands and wasn't trying to break bread with her own momma. After all the fucking cons and heists I pulled to get her everything she needed. I was feeling very unappreciated in her house. She's walking around with five thousand dollar purses and expensive ass shoes like it was nothing. Not one time did she offer me shit. In my opinion the bitch owed me. If it wasn't for me she wouldn't have even had that good life with that nigga Sheik. I should have kept his ass for myself. Being the dope ass mother that I am I decided to give him to my protégé. Had I known she was going to fall in love on the first date I never would have sent her ass.

The more I think about it I no longer feel fucked up about the shit. I earned every fucking dime. Plus, she's going to get all of that back anyway since she's selling her condo. The sound of my phone ringing made me roll my eyes. I knew it was Butch with his irritating ass. It was like this nigga didn't understand that I wasn't fucking with him like that. Now don't get me wrong Butch was the truth and always had money over the years. However, I always want the nigga with the fatter pockets.

Since Azada didn't want Trigga I hopped on that dick with no problem. I know its scandalous but a bitch got to do what a bitch got to do to survive. Azada definitely missed her beat with him. I'm sure by now Butch is well aware that I'm fucking with Trigga. I simply don't give a fuck about the way he feels either. Butch was old news it was time for me to get on some new shit. Trigga has the type of money a bitch needs to stay afloat. Butch probably would have had a better chance with me if he wasn't addicted to powder. I would do the shit here and there. Butch on the other hand needed that shit to function. My biggest problem was that he was always pushing that shit on me. I was a lot of things but a dope fiend wasn't about to be added to my resume. Fuck that. I needed a real nigga and Butch was not cutting it anymore.

I SAT up in bed in awe at the diamond tennis bracelet and necklace that Trigga had got for me. This nigga had spared no expense on me since we had started fucking around. Every time I turned around he was buying me gifts, taking me to extravagant restaurants, and tearing the mall down with no budget. Yeah this nigga definitely was a keeper. I was lying at the foot of the bed spent after the fuck session we just had. Azada crossed my mind so I grabbed my phone to call and check on her. Trigga grabbed my phone from my hand before I could dial her.

"I just wanted to call and check on my daughter that's all. She hasn't been answering her phone for me." Technically I hadn't been calling her because I knew she wouldn't answer. Trigga didn't have to know that though. You don't always have to let your right hand know what your left hand is doing. That's why he has no idea that I'm sitting on the money that I have. Shit, I'm trying spend all his shit up and move on to the next sucker.

"She's probably sleeping." He said as he flamed up a blunt and stared at me intensely.

"Why are you looking at me like that?"

"I'm just thinking about how you haven't properly thanked me for your gifts." I looked at him like he was crazy and started laughing.

"Baby, I've been fucking you like a porn star. That should be more than enough."

"Well it ain't enough. I need you to prove your loyalty to me. Get on your knees and crawl over here to me." That request was odd but I went along with it because I know in the long run the shit will pay off. As I crawled over to him I didn't like the way he looked. He had a vicious look in his eyes that mad me uneasy. However, I went with the flow and when I made it over to him I begin sucking his dick. I sucked and slobbed all over it until he was shooting his seeds down my throat.

"I fuck with you baby just let me know what you want me to do. I'll do it with no problem."

"That's a good girl. I'm putting some shit together right now. I'll let you know what I want you to do later. Right now I want you to turn around and toot that ass up." I cringed on the inside because this nigga wanted to fuck me in the ass. Now that I think about it he would rather do that than fuck this pussy. The shit was weird but for the money he was dishing out I would endure the pain.

24

SEVEN

Nightmares of being shot plagued me. It had been two months since the shooting and I was suffering from Post Traumatic Stress. Nothing prepared me for this shit. I wouldn't wish this shit on my worst enemy even if she was alive. Although Kimora was dead as fuck I still hated her. She had no idea what she had done to me. Besides shooting me she killed my unborn child. I know that I should be thanking God that I'm still in the land of the living but I'm angry. My ass is even angrier because that bitch died before I could get her back.

On top of that I'm dealing with Hussein being distant. It's like since the incident he hasn't really fucked with me like that. Prior to the incident he had basically moved in and now he barely stays the night. He has no idea what this is doing to me. I've been trying my best not to pressure him because I know he's fucked up behind the shit. However, I am too and I need for him to man the fuck up and be supportive. We both lost a baby. Just because we didn't know about the pregnancy prior doesn't make the shit hurt any less.

My bullet wound was healing but old wounds had resurfaced. My grandmother and father had been coming around since the shooting.

The last thing I wanted was a relationship with these people. I know my momma rolling over in her grave seeing what they did to me.

There was a time I loved my grandma but that changed when she failed to protect me. She caught my father on top of me. I was fighting with everything inside of me to keep him from raping me but he was too strong. She beat him with a broom and vowed to kill him if he she ever caught him fucking with me again. Instead of making him leave she allowed him to stay giving him all access to me. Even though she threatened him he didn't give a fuck. I used to wonder how he could live with himself knowing he wasn't right in the head. The saddest and sickest thing in the world is knowing your own father violated you like that.

The only reason they were at the hospital was because I was in the system and my grandmother was an emergency contact that I used years ago. I just wanted them to leave me alone. I been cut them out of my life and I want no parts of them now. I'm glad Yoka didn't tell Hussein about me being raped. I don't want him looking at me like damaged goods or with pity. I'm a different type of woman in regards to being a victim of child molestation. I don't dwell on it. I've grown from it all. Going to counseling made me realize that I didn't do anything wrong and they did everything wrong. I was a child and they were the adults. Counseling helped me to move on with my life and I'm content with that. As far as I'm concerned they can go back to Atlanta and forget I exist. I'm doing just fine without them.

The more I thought about Hussein distancing himself the angrier I became. There was a part of me that wanted to just say fuck it and let him have his space. While the other part of me wanted to go get him and make him come home. We haven't been through all of these changes to just not be here for one another. I love Hussein so much that I'm willing to fight for us. Getting shot will not be in vain. I'm going to get my man. If I have to drag his ass home I will.

~

"WHAT'S GOOD MA?" Hussein asked as I walked inside of his office at the reality company he shared with Sheik.

"Ain't shit good? Why the fuck you walking around acting like you not fucking with me? I'm over in that big ass house all by myself. Has something changed between us? If it has I think that I deserve to know.

"We good. I've just been trying to get my head together. A nigga ain't been on no bullshit with no bitches or nothing like that. This shit with you getting shot and Kimora killing herself has been too much." I had to take a step back and look at him.

"Yes, it has been all too much for me to bear as well but I am. The saddest part of it all is that I'm doing the shit alone. In case you forgot I was shot and the healing process has been hell on me mentally. Every night I wake up in cold sweats from the fucking nightmares I be having. You are not the only one who lost a baby I did too. You should be with me so that we can heal together but you're too self-centered for that. I initially came over here to drag your black ass home but I changed my mind. Stay your selfish ass here. I'll deal with this shit on my own like I've been doing. I love you and that won't change over night. However, I can't wait around forever for you to ride for me like I've been riding for you. With that being said I walked away from his ass I didn't want to hear anything else he was talking about. I was going to deal with this shit on my own. Fuck Hussein!

25

YOKA

Today was the day my baby was coming home and I was happy as hell. Sheik and I had been preparing for this day since the day he found out about her. At one point I thought she wasn't going to make it but she tricked us all. My daughter is strong just like me. I never thought that I would be this happy again. As much as it hurt to not have my mother here to experience being a grandmother I know that she's here with us in spirit. As I fixed my makeup in the mirror I realized I was finally comfortable with my hair again. It had grown back from when Zuri had cut it all off. Just the thought of him made me cringe. The nigga was just way to evil to be in the world with normal people.

"You ready yet babe?" Sheik peeked his head in the door and smiled at me. I blushed because he looks at me with so much admiration. It's like his eyes light up when I'm in his presence. Simply walking into a room makes him dote on me. It's weird but it feels so good at the same time. When you've been in a loveless and abusive relationship for so long the littlest form of attention from the opposite sex will have you smitten. Sheik tells me how beautiful I am and how much he loves me literally all day. Lord, knows I found my everything when we found each other.

"Yeah. I'm ready. I can't wait to put her on that Gucci outfit your momma got her. It's so cute."

"Don't put my baby in that fake shit. My momma ain't brought no real Gucci babe. One of her friends probably made that shit in their kitchen." Sheik laughed hard as hell but I didn't see shit funny. I couldn't tell if he was serious or not. At the same time banging on the front door caught both of our attention.

"Who could that be?"

"That's probably Hussein. He's the only one who got the heart to beat on my fucking door like that." We both walked to the door and when he opened we were both shocked looking at damn near the entire police force.

"Sheikem Shakur we have a warrant for your arrest."

"Fuck you mean you have a warrant for my arrest? I haven't did shit."

"Baby, what they talking about?" My heart was racing because the officer had took his cuffs out and was roughly putting his hands behind his back.

"That shit tight as fuck! What the fuck am I being arrested for this shit has got to be a mistake?"

"Azaka Shakur doesn't ring a bell?" The officer asked.

"Yeah! What about her?"

"You're the one killed her so you tell me. As a matter of fact save the shit for the judge."

"You got me fucked up!"

"Noooo! Sheik what are they talking about? Let him go we have to go get our daughter from the hospital.

"Calm down Yoka. This shit is all a misunderstanding I'll be out before you know it."

"You promised you would never leave us!" I didn't mean to sound so fucking weak but I had just got used to living our life together. Now up out of the blue he was going to jail. I couldn't do shit but panic.

"Aye! Wipe your motherfucking face! I don't want to see no more tears. You're my MVP! In case you don't know what that means it means Most Valuable Player. We're a team and I need you to be strong for the both of us. Go get my daughter and bring her home. I'll be here before you know it. Let me here you say you're my MVP! I need you to tell me that shit before they take my ass to jail!"

"I'm your MVP." I sniffled.

"Nah! Say that shit like you mean it. Make me a motherfucking believer!"

"I'm your MVP!" I yelled.

"That's my girl. Now come give me a kiss." I wrapped my arms around his neck and gave him a kiss. Seconds later he was been snatched away and placed in the back of the police car. I was so hurt I couldn't stand there and watch them drive away with him. Behind closed doors I cried my heart out. This shit couldn't be happening. Hearing him say I was his MVP in my head made me get my shit together and head to the hospital to grab my baby. I would get in contact with his momma and brother afterwards.

As I walked up to the hospital doors I was quickly stopped in my tracks by security.

"I'm sorry ma'am no on can come in or out."

"I have to come inside to get my daughter. She's being discharged from the NICU."

"That's why we're on lockdown a baby has been kidnapped." My heart stopped for a minute and I begin to panic. I reached inside my purse to grab my phone so that I could call her nurse but I had left it in the car on the charger. On my way towards the garage I noticed a woman in scrubs running with a baby in her arms. A car sped in front of her and opened the passenger door so she could get in. Something inside of me told me to speed walk in that direction. Before I could get closer it sped off but I did get a look at plate. My world crashed as I read ONEZU. It was Zuri. He always had that on his plates. I collapsed on the ground because I had come to the real- ization that this nigga had kidnapped my daughter.

TO BE CONTINUED!!!!

COMING SOON!!!

HOOD SUPREME:

The Santorini Crime Family

Written By:

Written By:Mz.Lady P

26

SAPPHIRE SANTORINI

People say that time heals all wounds but I don't think that shit is true at all. It's been a year since the death of my five year old son and I still can't seem to shake this Depression. My family thinks that I'm okay because I put on a brave face and continue to run the streets without a problem. The shit doesn't hit me until I'm home alone. I find myself sleeping in his superman bed just praying that he comes to me in my dreams. I smell his scent and I hear his laughter. Sometimes I've had to catch myself because I will call out his name. Reality sets in when I don't get a response.

A year ago my life was everything a bitch could ask for. Within the blink of an eye I lost my son and his father. I lost everything that was worth living for within the blink of an eye. I've always believed that God was real but where was God when my family was being murdered.

I still can hear my sister Ruby screaming and hollering talking about someone shot Dasani's car up with my son Dashon inside with him. For as long as I have breath in my body I'll spend my life trying to figure out who in the fuck was behind the shit.

The streets blame me because of my way of life but Dasani was no saint. He flipped bricks and held court in the streets. Quiet as it's kept the shit could have come from anywhere. There is no honor on the gritty streets of Chicago. These niggas don't care about taking lives. Everyone is expendable even innocent kids who have nothing to do with their parent's drug dealings.

A lone tear slid down my face as I thought of Dasani. He was my first everything. Growing up I was a tomboy but he fucked that shit right up out of me and I've been with that girly shit ever since. To this day my father still hasn't accepted the fact that I'm not the boy he was trying to groom me to be. Dasani made me look at life different and he made me want so much more out of life. When I became pregnant with his baby we made plans to live better and get out the game. That shit never came. They were murdered and I'm in the streets heavier than I ever was. I don't give a fuck these days. My main focus is all things that deal with my family.

~

THE SOUND of someone banging on my door made me quickly sit up in bed. I knew it couldn't be anyone but one of my sisters Ruby or Emerald. I've ignored their calls and texts all morning but as you can see they're determined to fuck with me today. It's Sunday and they know I'm off on Sundays. It's beyond me why after all this time they just don't get it. I work like a Hebrew slave all fucking week and I just need some me time. Sundays are my days to sulk and cry over the loss that I've endured. Quickly jumping up from bed I rushed to the front door to let them in. I didn't even bother to put my robe on. I answered the door in my bra and panties

"It's about time bitch. It's cold as fuck out there. What you in here doing playing with yourself. Where the hell ya clothes at?" Ruby said as she pushed passed me. I rolled my eyes because she was ignorant as fuck.

"Hey Big Sis. Get dressed. We're taking you out to lunch." Emerald came in and kissed me on the jaw. Now Emerald is the quiet and sweet one. She wouldn't hurt a fly unless she had to. Don't let her quietness fool you though. Sis is nice with her nine millimeter. I taught her well.

"Not today bitches. Y'all know Sunday is my rest day. Plus, it's Dasani's birthday. All I want to do is lay in bed and watch our old videos on his phone." I sat down on the sofa next to Ruby and snatched the blunt she had flamed up.

"Damn bitch! You need to get out and get you some much needed dick. It's been a year since Dasani passed and your ass is still sitting in this house sulking. Don't get me wrong I love my Bro but bitch you need to move on."

"Really Ru? Shut the fuck up!" Emerald yelled.

"Forgetting about Dasani would be like forgetting about Dashon. I'm just not ready to do that. Thanks for the invite but I'll take a rain check. I'll see you bitches at the trap bright and early in the morning. " I chucked up the deuces and headed back to my bedroom. I climbed under the covers and grabbed Dasani's old phone off the nightstand. It's crazy that I keep his phone charged up like he's going to need it. The more I sat crying my eyes out watching videos of us the more I realized how much I was driving myself crazy. I had been having so many regrets bout not spending more time with my son or not accepting Dasani's hand in marriage. It's true when they say that you need to love people while they're still here. I was not in a good head-space personally. In the streets I wore a brave face because I could never let my enemies see me weak. This mourning shit I was doing was unhealthy mentally. I live inside my home like they're still here. Sometimes I set the table like they're going to sit and eat dinner with me. Hell, I even cook big meals only to eat one plate and throw the rest away. If my sisters or my parents knew what I was doing they would probably commit me.

For the rest of the night I lay in bed and thought about my life. One thing for sure and two for certain there was no way I could live the rest of my life sulking. I closed my eyes and dreamed about the love of my life and my son. It's crazy but sometimes I can feel their presence like they're somewhere waiting to reunite with me. Then I remember I was at their funeral and I watched them get lowered into the ground. There is no coming back from that. My father Sergio Santorini fixes everything but this is something he can't fix and I have to deal with it. On the other hand he has given my sisters and I the key to Santorini Enterprises. It's time I boss up and take charge of the streets. Tomorrow will be the first day of the rest of my life. I'm Sapphire Santorini and I'm a motherfucking Boss!!

SUBSCRIBE

Text Shan to 22828 to stay up to date with new releases, sneak peeks, contest, and more...

WANT TO BE A PART OF SHAN PRESENTS?

To submit your manuscript to Shan Presents, please send the first three chapters and synopsis to submissions@shanpresents.com

Made in the USA
Lexington, KY
11 July 2018